# THE
## WOMEN'S MURDER CLUB
# TRIAL
# JAMES
# PATTERSON

### WITH *MAXINE PAETRO*

# BOOK**SHOTS**

1 3 5 7 9 10 8 6 4 2

BookShots
20 Vauxhall Bridge Road
London SW1V 2SA

BookShots is part of the Penguin Random House
group of companies whose addresses can be found at
global.penguinrandomhouse.com

Penguin
Random House
UK

First published by BookShots in 2016

www.penguin.co.uk

A CIP catalogue record for this book is available
from the British Library.

ISBN 9781786530257

Printed and bound in Great Britain by Clays Ltd, St Ives Plc

MIX
Paper from
responsible sources
FSC® C018179

Penguin Random House is committed to a sustainable future
for our business, our readers and our planet. This book is made
from Forest Stewardship Council® certified paper.

# THE WOMEN'S MURDER CLUB
# TRIAL

# CHAPTER 1

**IT WAS THAT CRAZY** period between Thanksgiving and Christmas when work overflowed, time raced, and there wasn't enough light between dawn and dusk to get everything done.

Still, our gang of four, what we call the Women's Murder Club, always had a spouse-free holiday get-together dinner of drinks and bar food.

Yuki Castellano had picked the place.

It was called Uncle Maxie's Top Hat and was a bar and grill that had been a fixture in the Financial District for 150 years. It was decked out with art deco prints and mirrors on the walls, and a large, neon-lit clock behind the bar dominated the room. Maxie's catered to men in smart suits and women in tight skirts and spike heels who wore good jewelry.

I liked the place and felt at home there in a Mickey Spillane kind of way. Case in point: I was wearing straight-legged pants, a blue gabardine blazer, a Glock in my shoulder holster, and flat lace-up shoes. I stood in the bar area, slowly turning my head as I looked around for my BFFs.

"Lindsay. Yo."

Cindy Thomas waved her hand from the table tucked under the spiral staircase. I waved back, moved toward the nook inside the cranny. Claire Washburn was wearing a trench coat over her scrubs, with a button on the lapel that read SUPPORT OUR TROOPS. She peeled off her coat and gave me a hug and a half.

Cindy was also in her work clothes: cords and a bulky sweater, with a peacoat slung over the back of her chair. If I'd ducked under the table, I'm sure I would have seen steel-toed boots. Cindy was a crime reporter of note, and she was wearing her on-the-job hound dog clothes.

She blew me a couple of kisses, and Yuki stood up to give me her seat and a jasmine-scented smack on the cheek. She had clearly come from court, where she worked as a pro bono defense attorney for the poor and hopeless. Still, she was dressed impeccably, in pinstripes and pearls.

I took the chair across from Claire. She sat between Cindy and Yuki with her back to the room, and we all scooched up to the smallish glass-and-chrome table.

If it hasn't been said, we four are a mutual heart, soul, and work society in which we share our cases and views of the legal system, as well as our personal lives. Right now the girls were worried about me.

Three of us were married—me, Claire, and Yuki—and Cindy had a standing offer of a ring and vows to be exchanged in Grace Cathedral. Until very recently you couldn't have found four more happily hooked-up women. Then the bottom fell out of my marriage to Joe Molinari, the father of my child and a man I shared everything with, including my secrets.

We had had it so good, we kissed and made up before our fights were over. It was the typical: "You are right." "No, you are!"

Then Joe went missing during possibly the worst weeks of my life.

I'm a homicide cop, and I know when someone is telling me the truth and when things do not add up.

Joe missing in action had not added up. Because of that I had worried almost to panic. Where was he? Why hadn't he checked in? Why were my calls bouncing off his full mailbox? Was he still alive?

As the crisscrossed threads of espionage, destruction, and mass murder were untangled, Joe finally made his curtain call with stories of his past and present lives that I'd never heard before. I found plenty of reason not to trust him anymore.

Even he would agree. I think anyone would.

It's not news that once trust is broken, it's damned hard to superglue it back together. And for me it might take more time and belief in Joe's confession than I actually had.

I still loved him. We'd shared a meal when he came to see our baby, Julie. We didn't make any moves toward getting divorced that night, but we didn't make love, either. Our relationship was now like the Cold War in the eighties between Russia and the USA, a strained but practical peace called détente.

Now, as I sat with my friends, I tried to put Joe out of my

mind, secure in the knowledge that my nanny was looking after Julie and that the home front was safe. I ordered a favorite holiday drink, a hot buttered rum, and a rare steak sandwich with Uncle Maxie's hot chili sauce.

My girlfriends were deep in criminal cross talk about Claire's holiday overload of corpses, Cindy's new cold case she'd exhumed from the *San Francisco Chronicle*'s dead letter files, and Yuki's hoped-for favorable verdict for her client, an underage drug dealer. I was almost caught up when Yuki said, "Linds, I gotta ask. Any Christmas plans with Joe?"

And that's when I was saved by the bell. My phone rang.

My friends said in unison, "NO PHONES."

It was the rule, but I'd forgotten—again.

I reached into my bag for my phone, saying, "Look, I'm turning it off."

But I saw that the call was from Rich Conklin, my partner and Cindy's fiancé. She recognized his ring tone on my phone.

"There goes our party," she said, tossing her napkin into the air.

"Linds?" said Conklin.

"Rich, can this wait? I'm in the middle—"

"It's Kingfisher. He's in a shoot-out with cops at the Vault. There've been casualties."

"But—Kingfisher is *dead*."

"Apparently, he's been resurrected."

# CHAPTER 2

**MY PARTNER WAS DOUBLE-PARKED** and waiting for me outside Uncle Maxie's, with the engine running and the flashers on. I got into the passenger seat of the unmarked car, and Richie handed me my vest. He's that way, like a younger version of a big brother. He thinks of me, watches out for me, and I try to do the same for him.

He watched me buckle up, then he hit the siren and stepped on the gas.

We were about five minutes from the Vault, a class A nightclub on the second floor of a former Bank of America building.

"Fill me in," I said to my partner.

"Call came in to 911 about ten minutes ago," Conklin said as we tore up California Street. "A kitchen worker said he recognized Kingfisher out in the bar. He was still trying to convince 911 that it was an emergency when shots were fired inside the club."

"Watch out on our right."

Richie yanked the wheel hard left to avoid an indecisive panel truck, then jerked it hard right and took a turn onto Sansome.

"You okay?" he asked.

I had been known to get carsick in jerky high-speed chases when I wasn't behind the wheel.

"I'm fine. Keep talking."

My partner told me that a second witness reported to first officers that three men were talking to two women at the bar. One of the men yelled, "No one screws with the King." Shots were fired. The women were killed.

"Caller didn't leave his name."

I was gripping both the dash and the door, and had both feet on imaginary brakes, but my mind was occupied with Kingfisher. He was a Mexican drug cartel boss, a psycho with a history of brutality and revenge, and a penchant for settling his scores personally.

Richie was saying, "Patrol units arrived as the shooters were attempting to flee through the front entrance. Someone saw the tattoo on the back of the hand of one of the shooters. I talked to Brady," Conklin said, referring to our lieutenant. "If that shooter is Kingfisher and survives, he's ours."

# CHAPTER 3

**I WANTED THE KING** on death row for the normal reasons. He was to the drug and murder trade as al-Baghdadi was to terrorism. But I also had personal reasons.

Earlier that year a cadre of dirty San Francisco cops from our division had taken down a number of drug houses for their own financial gain. One drug house in particular yielded a payoff of five to seven million in cash and drugs. Whether those cops knew it beforehand or not, the stolen loot belonged to Kingfisher—and he wanted it back.

The King took his revenge but was still short a big pile of dope and dollars.

So he turned his sights on me.

I was the primary homicide inspector on the dirty-cop case.

Using his own twisted logic, the King demanded that I personally recover and return his property. Or else.

It was a threat and a promise, and of course I couldn't deliver.

From that moment on I had protection all day and night, every day and night, but protection isn't enough when your tormentor is like a ghost. We had grainy photos and shoddy footage from cheap surveillance cameras on file. We had a blurry picture of a tattoo on the back of his left hand.

That was all.

After his threat I couldn't cross the street from my apartment to my car without fear that Kingfisher would drop me dead in the street.

A week after the first of many threatening phone calls, the calls stopped. A report came in from the Mexican federal police saying that they had turned up the King's body in a shallow grave in Baja. That's what they said.

I had wondered then if the King was really dead. If the freaking nightmare was truly over.

I had just about convinced myself that my family and I were safe. Now the breaking news confirmed that my gut reaction had been right. Either the Mexican police had lied, or the King had tricked them with a dead doppelganger buried in the sand.

A few minutes ago the King had been identified by a kitchen worker at the Vault. If true, why had he surfaced again in San Francisco? Why had he chosen to show his face in a nightclub filled with people? Why shoot two women inside that club? And my number one question: Could we bring him in alive and take him to trial?

*Please, God. Please.*

# CHAPTER 4

**OUR CAR RADIO WAS** barking, crackling, and squealing at a high pitch as cars were directed to the Vault, in the middle of the block on Walnut Street. Cruisers and ambulances screamed past us as Conklin and I closed in on the scene. I badged the cop at the perimeter, and immediately after, Rich backed our car into a gap in the pack of law enforcement vehicles, parking it across the street from the Vault.

The Vault was built of stone block. It had two centered large glass doors, now shattered, with a half-circular window across the doorframe. Flanking the doors were two tall windows, capped with demilune windows, glass also shot out.

Shooters inside the Vault were using the granite doorframe as a barricade as they leaned out and fired on the uniformed officers positioned behind their car doors.

Conklin and I got out of our car with our guns drawn and crouched beside our wheel wells. Adrenaline whipped my heart into a gallop. I watched everything with clear eyes, and yet my mind flooded with memories of past shoot-outs. I had been shot and almost died. All three of my partners had been shot, one of them fatally.

And now I had a baby at home.

A cop at the car to my left shouted, *"Christ!"*

Her gun spun out of her hand and she grabbed her shoulder as she dropped to the asphalt. Her partner ran to her, dragged her toward the rear of the car, and called in, "Officer down." Just then SWAT arrived in force with a small caravan of SUVs and a ballistic armored transport vehicle as big as a bus. The SWAT commander used his megaphone, calling to the shooters, who had slipped back behind the fortresslike walls of the Vault.

"All exits are blocked. There's nowhere to run, nowhere to hide. Toss out the guns, now."

The answer to the SWAT commander was a fusillade of gunfire that pinged against steel chassis. SWAT hit back with automatic weapons, and two men fell out of the doorway onto the pavement.

The shooting stopped, leaving an echoing silence.

The commander used his megaphone and called out, "You. Put your gun down and we won't shoot. Fair warning. We're coming in."

"WAIT. I give up," said an accented voice. "Hands up, see?"

"Come all the way out. Come to me," said the SWAT commander.

I could see him from where I stood.

The last of the shooters was a short man with a café au

lait complexion, a prominent nose, dark hair that was brushed back. He was wearing a well-cut suit with a blood-splattered white shirt as he came out through the doorway with his hands up.

Two guys in tactical gear grabbed him and slammed him over the hood of an SUV, then cuffed and arrested him.

The SWAT commander dismounted from the armored vehicle. I recognized him as Reg Covington. We'd worked together before. Conklin and I walked over to where Reg was standing beside the last of the shooters.

Covington said, "Boxer. Conklin. You know this guy?"

He stood the shooter up so I could get a good look at his face. I'd never met Kingfisher. I compared the real-life suspect with my memory of the fuzzy videos I'd seen of Jorge Sierra, a.k.a. the King.

"Let me see his hands," I said.

It was a miracle that my voice sounded steady, even to my own ears. I was sweating and my breathing was shallow. My gut told me that this was the man.

Covington twisted the prisoner's hands so that I could see the backs of them. On the suspect's left hand was the tattoo of a kingfisher, the same as the one in the photo in Kingfisher's slim file.

I said to our prisoner, "Mr. Sierra. I'm Sergeant Boxer. Do you need medical attention?"

"Mouth-to-mouth resuscitation, maybe."

Covington jerked him to his feet and said, "We'll take good care of him. Don't worry."

He marched the King to the waiting police wagon, and I watched as he was shackled and chained to the bar before the door was closed.

Covington slapped the side of the van, and it took off as CSI and the medical examiner's van moved in and SWAT thundered into the Vault to clear the scene.

# CHAPTER 5

**CONKLIN AND I JOINED** the patrol cops who were talking to the Vault's freaked-out customers, now milling nervously in the taped-off section of the street.

We wanted an eyewitness description of the shooter or shooters in the *act* of killing two women in the bar.

That's not what we got.

One by one and in pairs, they answered our questions about what they had seen. It all came down to statements like *I was under the table. I was in the bathroom. I wasn't wearing my glasses. I couldn't see the bar. I didn't look up until I heard screaming, and then I ran to the back.*

We noted the sparse statements, took names and contact info, and asked each person to call if something occurred to him or her later. I was handing out my card when a patrolman came over, saying, "Sergeant, this is Ryan Kelly. He tends bar here. Mr. Kelly says he watched a conversation escalate into the shooting."

*Thank God.*

Ryan Kelly was about twenty-five, with dark, spiky hair. His skin was pale with shock.

Conklin said, "Mr. Kelly, what can you tell us?"

Kelly didn't hesitate.

"Two women were at the bar, both knockouts, and they were into each other. Touching knees, hands, the like. The blonde was in her twenties, tight black dress, drinking wine coolers. The other was brunette, in her thirties but in great shape, drinking a Scotch on the rocks, in a white dress, or maybe it was beige.

"Three guys, looked Mexican, came over. They were dressed right, between forty and fifty, I'd say. The brunette saw their reflections in the backbar mirror and she jumped. Like, *Oh, my God.* Then she introduced the blonde as 'my friend Cameron.'"

The bartender was on a roll and needed no encouragement to keep talking. He said there had been some back-and-forth among the five people, that the brunette had been nervous but the short man with the combed-back hair had been super calm and played with her.

"Like he was glad to meet her friend," said Kelly. "He asked me to mix him a drink called a Pastinaca. Has five ingredients that have to be poured in layers, and I had no open elderflower. There was a new bottle under the bar. So I ducked down to find it among a shitload of other bottles.

"Then I heard someone say in a really strong voice, 'No one screws with the King.' Something like that. There's a shot, and another right after it. Loud *pop, pop.* And then a bunch more. I had, like, a heart attack and flattened out on the floor behind the bar. There was screaming like crazy. I stayed down until our manager found me and said, 'Come on. Get outta here.'"

I asked, "You didn't see who did the shooting?"

Kelly said, "No. Okay for me to go now? I've told this to about three of you. My wife is going nuts waiting for me at home."

We took Kelly's contact information, and when Covington signaled us that the Vault was clear, Conklin and I gloved up, stepped around the dead men, their spilled blood, guns, and spent shells in the doorway, and went inside.

# CHAPTER 6

**I KNEW THE VAULT'S** layout: the ground floor of the former bank had been converted into a high-end haberdashery. Access to the nightclub upstairs was by the elevators at the rear of the store.

Conklin and I took in the scene. Bloody shoe prints tracked across the marble floors. Toppled clothing racks and mannequins lay across the aisles, but nothing moved.

We crossed the floor with care and took an elevator to the second-floor club, the scene of the shooting and a forensics investigation disaster.

Tables and chairs had been overturned in the customers' rush toward the fire exit. There were no surveillance cameras, and the floor was tacky with spilled booze and blood.

We picked our way around abandoned personal property and over to the long, polished bar, where two women in expensive clothing lay dead. One, blond, had collapsed across the bar top, and the other, dark-haired, had fallen dead at her feet.

The lighting was soft and unfocused, but still, I could see that the blond woman had been shot between the eyes and had taken slugs in her chest and arms. The woman on the floor had a bullet hole through the draped white silk across her chest, and there was another in her neck.

"Both shot at close range," Richie said.

He plucked a beaded bag off the floor and opened it, and I did the same with the second bag, a metallic leather clutch.

According to their driver's licenses, the brunette was Lucille Alison Stone and the blonde was Cameron Whittaker. I took pictures, and then Conklin and I carefully cat-walked out of the bar the way we had come.

As we were leaving, we passed Charlie Clapper, our CSI director, coming in with his crew.

Clapper was a former homicide cop and always looked like he'd stepped out of a Grecian Formula commercial. Neat. Composed. With comb marks in his hair. Always thorough, never a grandstander, he was one of the SFPD's MVPs.

"What's your take?" he asked us.

"It was overkill," I said. "Two women were shot to death at point-blank range and then shot some more. Three men were reportedly seen talking to them before the shooting. Two of them are in your capable hands until Claire takes them. We have one alive, being booked now."

"The news is out. You think he's Kingfisher."

"Could be. I hope so. I really hope this is our lucky day."

# CHAPTER 7

**BEFORE THE MEDICAL EXAMINER** had retrieved the women's bodies, while CSI was beginning the staggering work involved in processing a bar full of fingerprints and spent brass and the guns, Conklin and I went back to the Hall of Justice and met with our lieutenant, Jackson Brady.

Brady was platinum blond, hard bodied, and chill, a former narcotics detective from Miami. He had proven his smarts and his astonishing bravery with the SFPD over the last couple of years and had been promoted quickly to run our homicide squad.

His corner office had once been mine, but being head of paperwork and manpower deployment didn't suit my temperament. I liked working crime on the street. I hadn't wanted to like Brady when he took the lieutenant job, but I couldn't help myself. He was tough but fair, and now he was married to my dear friend Yuki Castellano. Today I was very glad that Brady had a history in narcotics, homicide, and organized crime.

Conklin and I sat with him in his glass-walled office and told him what we knew. It would be days before autopsies were done and guns and bullets were matched up with dead bodies. But I was pretty sure that the guns would not be registered, there would be no prints on file, and law enforcement might never know who owned the weapons that killed those women.

I said, "Their car was found on Washington—stolen, of course. The two dead men had both Los Toros and Mala Sangre tats. We're waiting for ID from Mexican authorities. One of the dead women knew Kingfisher. Lucille Alison Stone. She lived on Balboa, the thirty-two hundred block. Has a record. Shoplifting twice and possession of marijuana, under twenty grams. She comes up as a known associate of Jorge Sierra. That's it for her."

"And the other woman? Whittaker?"

"According to the bartender, who read their body language, Whittaker might be the girlfriend's girlfriend. She's a schoolteacher. Has no record."

Brady said, "Barry Schein, ADA. You know him?"

"Yes," Conklin and I said in unison.

"He's on his way up here. We've got thirty-six hours to put together a case for the grand jury while they're still convened. If we don't indict our suspect pronto, the FBI is going to grab him away from us. Ready to take a crack at the man who would be King?"

"Be right back," I said.

The ladies' room was outside the squad room and down the hall. I went in, washed my face, rinsed out my mouth, reset my ponytail. Then I walked back out into the hallway where I could get a signal and called Mrs. Rose.

"Not a problem, Lindsay," said the sweet granny who lived across the hall and babysat Julie Anne. "We're watching the Travel Channel. The Hebrides. Scotland. There are ponies."

"Thanks a million," I told her.

I rejoined my colleagues.

"Ready," I said to Brady, Conklin, and Barry Schein, the new rising star of the DA's office. "No better time than now."

# CHAPTER 8

**WHEN KINGFISHER BEGAN HIS** campaign against me, I read everything I could find on him.

From the sparse reports and sightings I knew that the five-foot-six Mexican man who was now sitting in Interrogation 1 with his hands cuffed and chained to a hook on the table had been running drugs since before he was ten and had picked up the nickname Martin Pescador. That was Spanish for *kingfisher*, a small, bright-colored fishing bird with a prominent beak.

By the time Sierra was twenty, he was an officer in the Los Toros cartel, a savage paramilitary operation that specialized in drug sales up and down the West Coast and points east. Ten years later Kingfisher led a group of his followers in a coup, resulting in a bloody rout that left headless bodies from both sides decomposing in the desert.

Los Toros was the bigger loser, and the new cartel, led by Kingfisher, was called Mala Sangre, a.k.a. Bad Blood.

Along with routine beheadings and assassinations, Mala Sangre regularly stopped busloads of people traveling along a stretch of highway. The elderly and children were killed immediately. Young women were raped before execution, and the men were forced to fight each other to the death, gladiator style.

Kingfisher's publicity campaign worked. He owned the drug trade from the foot of Mexico to the head of Northern California. He became immensely rich and topped all of law enforcement's "Most Wanted" lists, but he rarely showed himself. He changed homes frequently and ran his business from a laptop and by burner phones, and the Mexican police were notoriously bought and paid for by his cartel.

It was said that he had conjugal visits with his wife, Elena, but she had eluded attempts to tail her to her husband's location.

I was thinking about that as I stood with Brady, Conklin, and Schein behind the mirrored glass of the interrogation room. We were quickly joined by chief of police Warren Jacobi and a half dozen interested narcotics and robbery inspectors who had reasonably given up hope of ever seeing Kingfisher in custody.

Now we had him but didn't own him.

Could we put together an indictable case in a day and a half? Or would the Feds walk all over us?

Normally, my partner was the good cop and I was the hardass. I liked when Richie took the lead and set a trusting tone, but Kingfisher and I had history. He'd threatened my life.

Rich opened the door to the interrogation room, and we took the chairs across from the probable mass killer.

No one was more primed to do this interrogation than me.

# CHAPTER 9

**THE KING LOOKED AS** common as dirt in his orange jumpsuit and chrome-plated bracelets. But he wasn't ordinary at all. I thought through my opening approach. I could play up to him, try to get on his side and beguile him with sympathy, a well-tested and successful interview technique. Or I could go badass.

In the end I pitched right down the center.

I looked him in the eyes and said, "Hello again, Mr. Sierra. The ID in your wallet says that you're Geraldo Rivera."

He smirked.

"That's cute. What's your real name?"

He smirked again.

"Okay if I call you Jorge Sierra? Facial recognition software says that's who you are."

"It's your party, Officer."

"That's Sergeant. Since it's my party, Mr. Sierra it is. How about we do this the easiest and best way. You answer some questions for me so we can all call it a night. You're tired. I'm tired. But the internet is crackling. FBI wants you, and so do the Mexican authorities, who are already working on extradition papers. They are salivating."

"Everyone loves me."

I put the driver's licenses of Lucille Stone and Cameron Whittaker on the table.

"What were your relationships to these two women?"

"They both look good to me, but I never saw either one of them before."

"Before tonight, you mean? We have a witness who saw you kill these women."

"Don't know them, never saw them."

I opened a folder and took out the 8½ x 11 photo of Lucille Stone lying across the bar. "She took four slugs to the chest, three more to the face."

"How do you say? Tragic."

"She was your lady friend, right?"

"I have a wife. I don't have lady friends."

"Elena Sierra. I hear she lives here in San Francisco with your two children."

No answer.

"And this woman," I said, taking out the print of the photo I'd taken of the blond-haired woman lying on the bar floor.

"Cameron Whittaker. I counted three or four bullet holes in her, but could be more."

His face was expressionless. "A complete stranger to me."

"Uh-huh. Our witness tells us that these two, your girlfriend and Ms. Whittaker, were very into each other. Kissing and the like."

Kingfisher scoffed. He truly looked amused. "I'm sorry I didn't see them. I might have enjoyed to watch. Anyway, they have nothing to do with me."

I pulled out CSI's photos of the two dead shooters. "These men. Could you identify them for us? They both have two sets of gang tats but have fake IDs on them. We'd like to notify their families."

No answer, but if Kingfisher gave a flip about them, you couldn't tell. I doubted a lie detector could tell.

As for me, my heart was still racing. I was aware of the men behind the glass, and I knew that if I screwed up this interrogation, I would let us all down.

I looked at Richie. He moved his chair a couple of inches back from the table, signaling me that he didn't want to insert himself into the conversation.

I tried a Richie-like tack.

"See it through my eyes, Mr. Sierra. You have blood spatter on your shirt. Spray, actually. The kind a person would *expel* onto you if she took a shot to the lung and you were standing right next to her. Your hands tested positive for gunpowder. There were a hundred witnesses. We've got three guns and a large number of slugs at our forensics lab, and they're all going to tell the same story. Any ADA drawn at random could get an indictment in less time than it takes for the judge to say 'No bail.'"

The little bird with the long beak smiled. I smiled back, then I said, "If you help us, Mr. Sierra, we'll tell the DA you've been cooperative. Maybe we can work it so you spend your time in the supermax prison of your choice. Currently, although it could change in the near future, capital punishment is illegal in California. You can't be extradited to Mexico until you've served your sentence here. Good chance that will never happen, you understand? But you will get to *live*."

"I need to use the phone," Kingfisher said.

I saw the brick wall directly up ahead. I ignored the request for a phone and kept talking.

"Or we don't fight the extradition warrant. You take the prison shuttle down to Mexico City and let the *federales* talk to you about many mass murders. Though, frankly, I don't see you surviving long enough in Mexico to even get to trial."

"You didn't hear me?" our prisoner asked. "I want to call my lawyer."

Richie and I stood up and opened the door for the two jail guards, who came in and took him back to his cell.

Back in the viewing room Conklin said, "You did everything possible, Linds."

The other men uttered versions of "Too bad" and left me alone with Conklin, Jacobi, Brady, and young Mr. Schein.

I said, "He's not going to confess. We've got nothing. To state the obvious, people are afraid of him, so we have no witnesses. We don't know if he's the killer, or even if he is the King."

"Find out," said Brady. He had a slight southern drawl, so it came out "Fahnd out."

We all got the message.

Meeting over.

# CHAPTER 10

**IT WAS JUST AFTER** 8:00 p.m. when I walked into the apartment where Julie and I live. It's on Lake Street, not too far from the park.

Mrs. Rose, Julie's nanny, was snoozing on the big leather sofa, and our HDTV was on mute. Martha, my border collie and dear old friend, jumped to her feet and charged at me, woofing and leaping, overcome with joy.

Mrs. Rose swung her feet to the floor, and Julie let out a wail from her little room.

There was no place like home.

I spent a good hour cuddling with my little girl, chowing down on Gloria Rose's famous three-protein meat loaf, downing a couple of glasses of Pinot Noir, and giving Martha a back rub.

Once the place was tidy, the baby was asleep, and Mrs. Rose had left for the night, I opened my computer and e-mail.

First up, Charlie Clapper's ballistics report.

"Three guns recovered, all snubbies," he wrote, meaning short-barreled .38 Saturday night specials. "Bullets used were soft lead. Squashed to putty, every one of them, no striations. Fingerprints on the guns and shells match the two dead men and the man you booked, identity uncertain. Tats on the dead men are the usual prison-ink variety, with death heads and so forth, and they have both the Los Toros bull insignia and lettering saying *Mala Sangre*. Photos on file."

Charlie's report went on.

"Blood on the clothing of the dead men and your suspect is a match to the blood of the victims positively identified as Cameron Whittaker, white, twenty-five, grade-school substitute teacher, and Lucille Stone, white, twenty-eight. ID says she was VP of marketing at Solar Juice, a software firm in the city of Sunnyvale.

"That's all I've got, Lindsay. Sorry I don't have better news. Chas."

I phoned Richie, and Cindy picked up.

My reporter friend was a cross between an adorable, girly journalist and a pit bull, so she said, "I want to work on this Kingfisher story, Linds. Tell Rich it's okay for him to shar e with me."

I snorted a laugh, then said, "May I speak with him?"

"Will you? Share?"

"Not yet. We'll see."

"Fine," Cindy huffed. "Thanks."

Richie got on the phone.

He said, "I've got something that could lead to motive."

"Tell me."

"I spoke with the girlfriend's mother. She says Lucy was seeing

Sierra but broke it off with him about a month ago. Right after that Lucy believed that Sierra was dead. I mean, we all did, right?"

"Correct."

"According to Lucy Stone's mother, Sierra went to Lucy's apartment yesterday and Lucy wouldn't let him in. Mrs. Stone said her daughter called her and told her that Sierra was angry and threatening. Apparently, Lucy was afraid."

"He could have staked her out. Followed her to the Vault."

"Probably, yeah. I asked Mrs. Stone if she could ID Sierra. And she said—"

"Let me guess. 'No.'"

"Bingo. However…"

"Don't tease me, Richie."

He laughed. "Here ya go. Mrs. Stone said that the King's wife, Elena Sierra, has been living under the name Maura Steele. I got her number and address on Nob Hill."

*A lead. An actual lead.*

I told Richie he was the greatest. He laughed again. Must be nice to have such a sunny disposition.

After hanging up, I checked the locks on the door and windows, double-checked the alarm, looked in on my darling Julie, and put my gun on my night table.

I whistled for Martha.

She bounded into the bedroom and onto the bed.

"Night-night, sweet Martha."

I turned off the light and tried to sleep.

# CHAPTER 11

**WE MET IN THE** squad's break room the next morning: Conklin, Brady, ADA Schein, and me.

Schein was thirty-six, married, and a father of two. He reported directly to DA Len "Red Dog" Parisi, and he'd been pitching no-hitters since he took the job, sending the accused to jail every time he took the mound. Putting Kingfisher away would be Schein's ticket to a five-star law firm if he wanted it. He was suited up for the next big thing even now, close shaved and natty in this shabby setting, and he was all business. I liked it. I liked him.

Schein said, "Summarizing what we have: A 911 tape of a male with a Spanish accent reporting that he's seen Kingfisher at the Vault, and we presume that that's the man we arrested. The tipster said he was a kitchen worker but could have been anyone. He called from a burner phone, and this witness hasn't stepped forward."

Conklin and I nodded. Schein went on.

"We have a witness who saw the run-up to the shooting but didn't see the actual event."

I said, "We've got blood on the suspect's shirt."

"Good. But a juror is going to ask if he could have gotten that blood spray if he was near the victim but he didn't fire the weapon."

Schein shrugged. "What can I say. Yeah. Bottom line, twenty-four hours from now we get a 'proceed to prosecution' from the grand jury, or our suspect goes out of our hands and into the lap of a higher or different jurisdiction."

"Spell out exactly what you need," said Brady. He was making a list with a red grease pencil on a lined yellow pad.

"We need legally sufficient evidence and probable cause," said Schein. "And I can be persuasive up to a point."

"We have to positively ID our man as Jorge Sierra?"

"That's the price of admission. Without that, no hearing."

"Additionally," said Brady, "we get a witness to the shooting or to Sierra's intent to kill."

"That would nail it."

When the coffee containers and doughnut box were in the trash and we were alone at last, Rich said, "Cindy should run it in the *Chron* online."

"Like, 'SFPD needs info from anyone who was at the Vault on Wednesday night and saw the shooting'?"

"Yep," said Rich. "It's worked before."

# CHAPTER 12

**RICH WENT BACK TO** the crime scene for another look, and I called the former Mrs. Jorge Sierra, now Ms. Maura Steele. She didn't answer the phone, so I signed out a squad car and drove to her address in Nob Hill.

I badged the doorman and asked him to ring up to Ms. Sierra-a.k.a.-Steele's apartment.

He said, "You just missed her."

"This is important police business," I said. "Where can I find her?"

"She went to the gym. She usually gets back at around ten o'clock."

It was quarter to. I took a seat in a wingback chair with a view of the street through two-story-tall plate-glass windows and saw the black limo stop at the curb. A liveried driver got out, went around to the sidewalk side of the car, and opened the rear door.

A very attractive woman in her late twenties or early thirties got out and headed toward the lobby doors while she went for the keys in her bag.

Ms. Steele was slim and fine boned, with short, dark, curly

hair. She wore a smart shearling coat over her red tracksuit. I shot a look at the doorman and he nodded. When she came through the door, I introduced myself and showed her my badge.

"Police? What's this about?"

"Jorge Sierra," I said.

She drew back. Fear flickered in her eyes, and her face tightened.

She said, "I don't know anyone by that name."

"Please, Ms. Steele. Don't make me take you to the station for questioning. I just need you to ID a photograph."

The doorman was fiddling with papers at the front desk, trying to look as though he wasn't paying attention. He looked like Matt Damon but didn't have Damon's talent.

"Come upstairs with me," Ms. Steele said to me.

I followed her into the elevator, which opened directly into her sumptuous apartment. It was almost blindingly luxurious, with its Persian carpets, expensive furnishings, and what looked to me like good art against a backdrop of the Golden Gate Bridge and San Francisco Bay.

I'd looked her up before getting into the car. Ms. Steele didn't have a job now and had no listing under Sierra or Steele on LinkedIn, Facebook, or Who's Who in Business. Odds were, she was living on the spoils of her marriage to one of the richest men west of the Rockies.

Steele didn't ask me to sit down.

"I want to be absolutely clear," she said. "If you quote me or depose me or in any way try to put me on the record, I will deny everything. I'm still married. I can't testify."

I took the mug shot out of my pocket and held it up for her to see. "Is this Jorge Sierra?" I asked. "Known as Kingfisher?"

She began nodding like a bobblehead on crack. I can't say I didn't understand her terror. I'd felt something like it myself.

I said, "Thank you."

I asked follow-up questions as she walked with me back toward the elevator door. Had her husband been in touch with her? When was the last time she'd spoken with him? Any idea why he would have killed two women in a nightclub?

She stopped moving and answered only the last question.

"Because he is *crazy*. Because he is *mental* when it comes to women. I tried to leave him and make a run for the US border, but when he caught me, he did this."

She lifted her top so that her torso was exposed. There was a large scar on her body, about fifteen inches wide by ten inches long, shirring her skin from under her breasts to her navel. It looked like a burn made by a white-hot iron in the shape of a particular bird with a prominent beak. A kingfisher.

"He wanted any man I ever met to know that I belonged to him. Don't forget your promise. And don't let him go. If he gets out, call me. Okay?"

"Deal," I said. "That's a deal."

# CHAPTER 13

**EARLY FRIDAY MORNING CONKLIN** and I met with ADA Barry Schein in his office on the second floor of the Hall. He paced and flexed his hands. He was gunning his engines, which was to be expected. This was a hugely important grand jury hearing, and the weight of it was all on Barry.

"I'm going to try something a little risky," he said.

Barry spent a few minutes reviewing what we already knew about the grand jury—that it was a tool for the DA, a way to try out the case with a large jury in an informal setting to see if there was enough probable cause to indict. If the jury indicted Mr. Sierra, Schein could skip arraignment and take Sierra directly to trial.

"That's what we want," said Barry. "Speed."

Rich and I nodded that we got that.

Schein said, "There's no judge, no attorney for the defense, as you know. Just me and the jury," Schein said. "Right now we don't have sufficient evidence to indict Sierra on a murder of any degree. We can place him at the scene of the crime, but no one saw him fire his gun, and the forensics are inconclusive."

I said, "I'm ready to hear about your 'risky' move."

Schein straightened his tie, patted down his thinning hair, and said, "I've subpoenaed Sierra. This is rarely done, because the putative defendant is unlikely to testify against himself.

"That said, Sierra *has* to take the stand. Like most people in this spot, he'll plead the Fifth. So I'm going to try to use that to help us."

"How so?" I asked.

Schein cracked his first smile of the day.

"I'll lay out my case to the jury by asking Sierra: 'You had a plan in mind when you went to the Vault on the fourteenth, isn't that right? Lucille Stone was your girlfriend, correct, sir? But she rejected you, didn't she? You followed her and learned that she was involved with a woman, isn't that right, Mr. Sierra? Is that why you murdered her and Cameron Whittaker?'"

I didn't have to ask Schein to go on. He was still circling his office, talking from the game plan in his head.

"The more he refuses to answer," Schein said, "the more probable cause is raised in the jurors' minds. Could it backfire? Yeah. If the jury doesn't hold his refusal to testify against him, they'll hand me my hat. But we won't be any worse off than we are now."

An hour later Rich and I were in the San Francisco Superior Court on McAllister Street, benched in the hallway. Sierra had been brought into the courtroom through a back door, and as I'd seen when the front doors opened a crack, he was wearing street clothes, had shackles around his ankles, and was sitting between two hard-boiled marshals with guns on their hips.

Sierra's attorney, J. C. Fuentes, sat alone on a bench ten yards from where I sat with my partner. He was a huge, brutish-looking man of about fifty wearing an old brown suit. I knew him to be a winning criminal defense attorney. He wasn't an orator, but he was a remarkable strategist and tactician.

Today, like the rest of us, he was permitted only to wait outside the courtroom and to be available if his client needed to consult with him.

Rich plugged into his iPad and leaned back against the wall. I jiggled my feet, people-watched, and waited for news. I was unprepared when the courtroom doors violently burst open.

I jumped to my feet.

Jorge Sierra, still in chains, was being pulled and dragged out of the courtroom and into the hallway, where Mr. Fuentes, Conklin, and I stood, openmouthed and in shock.

Sierra shouted over his shoulder through the open doors.

"I have all your names, stupid people. I know where you live. Street addresses. Apartment layouts. You and your pathetic families can expect a visit very soon."

The doors swung closed and Fuentes rushed to Sierra's side as he was hauled past us, laughing his face off.

It was twenty past twelve. Rich said to me, "How long do you think before the jury comes back?"

I had no answer, not even a guess.

Fourteen minutes later Schein came out of the courtroom looking like he'd been through a wood chipper.

He said, "Sierra took the Fifth, and the jurors didn't like him. Before he got off the stand, he threatened them, and he didn't quit until the doors closed on his ass. Did you hear him? Threatening the jurors is another crime."

Rich said, "When do they decide, Barry?"

Schein said, "It's done. Unanimous decision. Sierra is indicted on two counts of murder one."

We pumped Schein's hand. The indictment gave us the time we needed to gather more evidence before Sierra went to trial. Conklin and I went back to the Hall to brief Brady.

"There is a God," Brady said, rising to his feet.

We high-fived over his desk, and Conklin said, "Break out the Bud."

It was a great moment. The Feds and the Mexican government had to step back. Jorge Sierra had been indicted for murder in California.

The King was in our jail and he was ours to convict.

# CHAPTER 14

**JOE AND I WERE** dancing together close and slow. He had his hand at the small of my back, and the hem of my low-cut slinky red gown swished around my ankles. I couldn't even feel my feet because I was dancing on cotton candy clouds. I felt so good in Joe's arms—loved, protected, and excited, too. I didn't want this dance to ever end.

"I miss you so much," he said into my ear.

I pulled back so I could look into his handsome face, his blue eyes. "I miss you—"

I never got out the last word.

My phone was singing with Brady's ring tone, a bugle call.

I grabbed for the phone, but it slipped out of my hand. Still half under the covers, I reached for it again, and by that time Martha was snuffling my face.

*God!*

"Boxer," I croaked.

Brady's voice was taut.

"A juror was found dead in the street. Gunned down."

I said, "No."

He said, "'Fraid so."

He told me to get on it, and I called Richie.

It was Saturday. Mrs. Rose was off, but I called her anyway. She sounded both half asleep and resigned but said, "I'll be right there."

She crossed the hall in her robe and slippers and asked if I wouldn't mind taking Martha out before I took off.

After a three-minute successful dog walk I guzzled coffee, put down a PowerBar, and drove to Chestnut Street, the main drag through the Marina District. This area was densely lined with restaurants and boutiques, normally swarming with young professionals, parents with strollers, and twentysomethings in yoga pants.

All that free-spirited weekend-morning traffic had come to a dead halt. A crowd of onlookers had formed a deep circle at the barrier tape enclosing a section of street and the victim's body.

I held up my badge and elbowed my way through to where Conklin was talking to the first officer, Sam Rocco.

Rocco said, "Sergeant, I was telling Conklin, a 911 caller reported that one of the grand jurors in the Sierra jury had been 'put down like a dog.'

"The operator said the caller sounded threatening. She got the street and cross street before the caller hung up," Rocco continued. "Feldman and I were here inside of five minutes. I opened the victim's wallet and got her particulars. Sarah Brenner. Lives two blocks over on Greenwich Street. From the coffee container in the gutter, looks like she was just coming back from Peet's on Chestnut."

"Anyone see the shooting?" I asked.

"None that will admit to it," said Officer Rocco.

"Cash and cards in the wallet?"

"Yep, and she's wearing a gold necklace and a watch."

Not a robbery. I thanked Rocco and edged around the dead body of a young woman who was lying facedown between two parked cars. She wore jeans and a green down jacket with down puffing out of its bullet holes, and nearby lay the slip-on mules that had been blown off her socked feet by the impact or the fall. Shell casings were scattered on the asphalt around the body, and some glinted from underneath the parked cars.

I lifted a strand of Sarah Brenner's long brown hair away from her face so that I could see her features. She looked sweet. And too young. I touched her neck to be sure she was really gone. *Goddamnit.*

Putting Sarah Brenner "down like a dog" was a crude term for a professional hit meant to scare everyone connected with Sierra's trial. Inciting fear. Payback. Revenge.

It was just Kingfisher's style.

I thought he might get away with killing this young woman as he had done so many times before. He would hit and run again.

# CHAPTER 15

**MONDAY MORNING RICH AND** I reported to Brady what we had learned that weekend.

Rich said, "Sarah was twenty-five, took violin lessons at night, did paperwork for a dentist during the day. She had no boyfriend, no recent ex, and lived with two other young women and an African gray parrot. She had a thousand and twenty dollars in the bank and a fifty-dollar credit card balance for a green down jacket. No enemies, only friends, none known to have a motive for her killing."

"Your thoughts?" Brady asked me.

"Maybe the King would like to brag."

Brady gave me a rare grin. "Knock yourself out," he said.

I took the stairs from our floor, four, to maximum security on seven. I checked in at the desk and was escorted to Sierra's brightly lit, windowless cell.

I stood a good five feet from the bars of the King's cage.

He looked like someone had roughed him up, and the orange jumpsuit did nothing for his coloring. He didn't look like the king of anything.

He stood up when he saw me, saying, "Well, hello, Officer Lindsay. You're not wearing lipstick. You didn't want to look nice for me?"

I ignored the taunt.

"How's it going?" I asked him.

I was hoping he had some complaints, that he wanted a window or a blanket—anything that I could use to barter for answers to questions that could lead to evidence against him.

He said, "Pretty good. Thank you for getting me a single room. I will be reasonably comfortable here. Not so much everyone else. That includes you, your baby girl, even your runaround husband, Joseph. Do you know who Joseph is sleeping with now? I do. Do you want to see the pictures? I can have them e-mailed to you."

It was a direct shot to the heart and caught me off guard. I struggled to keep my composure.

"How are you going to do that?" I asked.

Sierra had an unpleasant, high-pitched laugh.

I'd misjudged him. He had taken control of this meeting and I would learn nothing from him about Sarah Brenner—or about anyone else. The flush rising from under my collar let both of us know that he'd won the round.

I left Jorge Sierra, that disgusting load of rat dung, and jogged down the stairs to the squad room, muttering, promising myself that the next point would be mine.

Conklin and I sat near the front of the room. We'd pushed

our desks together so that we faced each other, and I saw that Cindy was sitting in my chair and Conklin was in his own. There were open Chinese food cartons between them.

I said hello to Cindy. Conklin dragged up a chair for her and I dropped into mine.

"Nice of you to bring lunch," I said, looking at the containers. I had no appetite whatsoever. Definitely not for shrimp with lobster sauce. Not even for tea.

"I've brought you something even nicer," she said, holding up a little black SIM card, like from a mobile phone.

"What's that?"

"This is a ray of golden sunshine breaking through the bleak skies overhead."

"Make me a believer," I said.

"A witness dropped this off at the *Chron* for me this morning," Cindy said. "It's a video of the shooting at the Vault's bar. You can see the gun in the King's hand. You can see the muzzle aimed at Lucy Stone's chest. You can see the flare after he pulled the trigger."

"This is evidence of Sierra shooting Stone on film?"

She gave me a Cheshire cat smile.

"The person who shot this video has a name?"

"Name, number, and is willing to testify."

"I love you, Cindy."

"I know."

"I mean I *really* love you."

Cindy and Rich burst out laughing, and after a stunned beat I laughed, too. We looked at the video together. It was good. We had direct evidence and a witness. Jorge Sierra was cooked.

# FOUR MONTHS LATER

# CHAPTER 16

**NO MATTER WHAT KIND** of crappy day life dealt out, it was almost impossible to sustain a bad mood at Susie's Café.

I parked my car on Jackson Street, buttoned my coat, and lowered my head against the cold April wind as I trudged toward the brightly lit Caribbean-style eatery frequented by the Women's Murder Club.

My feet knew the way, which was good, because my mind was elsewhere. Kingfisher's trial was starting tomorrow.

The media's interest in him had been revived, and news outlets of all kinds had gone on high alert. Traffic on Bryant and all around the Hall had been jammed all week with satellite vans. None of my phones had stopped ringing: office, home, or mobile.

I felt brittle and edgy as I went through the front door of Susie's. I was first to arrive and claimed "our" booth in the back room. I signaled to Lorraine and she brought me a tall, icy brewski, and pretty soon that golden anesthetic had smoothed down my edges.

Just about then I heard Yuki and Cindy bantering together

and saw the two of them heading toward our table. There were kiss-kisses all around, then two of my blood sisters slid onto the banquette across from me.

Cindy ordered a beer and Yuki ordered a Grasshopper, a frothy green drink that would send her to the moon, and she always enjoyed the flight. So did the rest of us.

Cindy told me that Claire had phoned to say she would be late, and once Cindy had downed some of my beer, she said, "I've got news."

Cindy, like every other reporter in the world, was covering the Sierra trial. But she was a crime pro and the story was happening on her beat. Other papers were running her stories under her byline. That was good for Cindy, and I could see from the bloom in her cheeks that she was on an adrenaline high.

She leaned in and spoke only loud enough to be heard over the steel drums in the front room and the laughter at the tables around ours.

She said, "I got an anonymous e-mail saying that 'something dramatic' is going to happen if the charges against Sierra aren't dismissed."

"Dramatic how?" I asked.

"Don't know," Cindy said. "But I could find out. Apparently, the King wants me to interview him."

Cindy's book about a pair of serial killers had swept to the top of the bestseller lists last year. Sierra could have heard about her. He might be a fan.

I reached across the table and clasped Cindy's hands.

"Cindy, do not even think about it. You don't want this man to know anything about you. I oughta know."

"For the first time since I met you," Cindy said, "I'm going to say you are right. I'm not asking to see him. I'm going to just walk away."

I said, "Thank you, God."

Lorraine brought Cindy her beer, and Yuki took the floor.

She said almost wistfully, "I know Barry Schein pretty well. Worked with him for a couple of years. If anyone can handle the King's drama, it's Barry. I admire him. He could get Red Dog's job one day."

None of us would ever forget this very typical night at Susie's. Before we left the table, it would be permanently engraved in our collective memories. We were chowing down on Susie's Sunday-night special, fish fritters and rice, when my phone tootled. I had left it on only in case Claire called saying she wasn't going to make it. But it was Brady's ring tone that came through.

I took the call.

Brady gave me very bad news. I told him I was on my way and clicked off. I repeated the shocking bulletin to Cindy and Yuki. We hugged wordlessly.

Then I bolted for my car.

# CHAPTER 17

**FROM THE LOOK OF** it, the Scheins lived in a classic American dream home, a lovely Cape Cod on Pachecho Street in Golden Gate Heights with a princely view, two late-model cars, a grassy yard, and a tree with a swing.

Today, Pacheco Street was taped off. Cruisers with cherry flashers marked the perimeter, and halogen lights illuminated an evidence tent and three thousand square feet of pavement.

The first officer, Donnie Lewis, lifted the tape and let me onto the scene.

Normally cool, the flustered CSI director, Clapper, came toward me, saying, "Jesus, Boxer, brace yourself. This is brutal."

My skin prickled and my stomach heaved as Clapper walked me to the Scheins' driveway, which sloped down from the street to the attached garage. Barry's body was lying faceup, eyes open, keys in his hand, the door to his silver-blue Honda Civic wide open.

I lost my place in time. The pavement shifted underfoot and the whole world went cold. I covered my face with my hands, felt Clapper's arm around my shoulders. "I'm here, Lindsay. I'm here."

I took my hands down and said to Clapper, "I just spoke with him yesterday. He was ready to go to trial. He was ready, Charlie."

"I know. I know. It never makes sense."

I stared down at Barry's body. There were too many holes punched in his jacket for me to count. Blood had outlined his body and was running in rivulets down toward the garage.

I dropped enough f-bombs to be seen on the moon.

And then I asked Clapper to fill me in.

"The little boy was running down the steps right there to greet his father. Daddy was calling to the kid, then he turned back toward the street. Must have heard the shooter's car pull up, or maybe his name was called. He turned to see—and was gunned down."

"How old is the child?"

"Four. His name is Stevie."

"Could he describe what he saw?" I asked Clapper.

"He told Officer Lewis that he saw a car stop about here on the road at the top of the driveway. He heard the shots, saw his father drop. He turned and ran back up the steps and inside. Then, according to Lewis, Barry's wife, Melanie, she came out. She tried to resuscitate her husband. Their daughter, Carol, age six, ran away to the house next door. Her best friend lives there.

"Melanie and Stevie are in the house until we can get all of them out of here."

"What's your take?" I asked Clapper.

"Either the driver tailed the victim, or he parked nearby, saw

Schein's car drive past, and followed him. When Barry got out of the car, the passenger emptied his load. Barry never had a chance."

We stepped away from the body, and CSIs deployed in full. Cameras clicked, video rolled, and a sketch artist laid out the details of the crime scene from a bird's-eye point of view. Techs searched for and located shell casings, put markers down, took more pictures, brought shell casings to the tent.

Conklin said, "Oh, my God."

I hadn't heard him arrive but I was so glad to see him. We hugged, hung on for a minute. Then we stood together in the sharp white light, looking down at Barry's body lying at our feet. We couldn't look away.

Rich said, "Barry told me that when this was over, he was taking the kids to Myrtle Beach. There's family there."

I said, "He told me he'd waited his whole career for a case like this. He told me he was going to wear his lucky tiepin. Belonged to his grandfather."

My partner said, "Kingfisher put out the hit. Had to be. I wish I could ask Barry if he saw the shooter."

I answered with a nod.

Together we mounted the brick front steps to the white clapboard house with black shutters, the remains of the Schein family's life as they had known it.

Now a couple of cops were going to talk to this family in the worst hour of their lives.

# CHAPTER 18

**WE RANG THE FRONT** doorbell. We knocked. We rang the bell again before Melanie Schein, a distraught woman in her midthirties, opened the front door.

She looked past us and spoke in a frantic, disbelieving voice. "My God, my God, this can't be true. We're having chicken and potatoes. Barry likes the dark meat. I got ice cream pie. We picked out a movie."

Richie introduced us, said how sorry we were, that we knew Barry, that this was our case.

"We're devastated," Richie said.

But I don't think Barry's wife heard us.

She turned away from the door, and we followed her into the aromatic kitchen and, from there, into the living room. She looked around at her things and bent to line up the toes of a pair of men's slippers in front of a reclining chair.

I asked her the questions I knew by heart.

"Do you have a security camera?"

She shook her head.

"Has either of you received any threats?"

"I want to go to him. I need be with him."

"Has anyone threatened you or Barry, Mrs. Schein?"

She shook her head. Tears flew off her cheeks.

I wanted to give her something, but all I had were rules and platitudes and a promise to find Barry's killer. It was a promise I wasn't sure we could keep.

I promised anyway. And then I said, "Witness Protection will be here in a few minutes to take you and the children to a safe place. But first, could we talk with Stevie for just a minute?"

Mrs. Schein led us down a hallway lined with framed family photos on the walls. Wedding pictures. Baby pictures. The little girl on a pony. Stevie with an oversized catcher's mitt.

It was almost impossible to reconcile this hominess with the truth of Barry's still-warm body lying outside in the cold. Mrs. Schein asked us to wait, and when she opened the bedroom door, I was struck by the red lights flashing through the curtains. A little boy sat on the floor, pushing a toy truck back and forth mindlessly. What did he understand about what had happened to his father? I couldn't shake the thought that an hour ago Barry had been alive.

With Mrs. Schein's permission Richie went into the room and stooped beside the child. He spoke softly, but we could all hear his questions: "Stevie, did you see a car, a truck, or an SUV?…Car? What color car?…Have you seen it before?…Did you recognize the man who fired the gun?…Can you describe him at all?…Is there anything you want to tell me? I'm the police, Stevie. I'm here to help."

Stevie said again, "Was a gray car."

Conklin asked, "How many doors, Stevie? Try to picture it." But Stevie was done. Conklin opened his arms and Stevie collapsed against him and sobbed.

I told Mrs. Schein to call either of us anytime. Please.

After giving her our cards, my partner and I took the steps down to the halogen-lit hell in front of the lovely house.

In the last ten minutes the street had thickened with frightened neighbors, frustrated motorists, and cops doing traffic control. The medical examiner's van was parked inside the cordoned-off area of the street.

Dr. Claire Washburn, chief medical examiner and my dearest friend, was supervising the removal of Barry Schein's bagged body into the back of her van.

I went to her and she grabbed my hands.

"God-awful shame. That talented young man. The doer made damned sure he was dead," said Claire. "What a waste. You okay, Lindsay?"

"Not really."

Claire and I agreed to speak later. The rear doors to the coroner's van slammed shut and the vehicle took off. I was looking for Conklin when an enormous, pear-shaped man I knew very well ducked under the tape and cast his shadow over the scene.

Leonard Parisi was San Francisco's district attorney. He wasn't just physically imposing, he was a career prosecutor with a long record of wins.

"This is…abominable," said Parisi.

"Fucking tragedy," Conklin said, his voice cracking.

I said, "I'm so sorry, Len. We're about to canvass. Maybe someone saw something. Maybe a camera caught a license plate."

Parisi nodded. "I'm getting a continuance on the trial," he said. "I'm taking over for Barry. I'm going to make Kingfisher wish he were dead."

# CHAPTER 19

**A WEEK HAD PASSED** since Barry Schein was killed fifteen hours before Sierra's trial had been scheduled to begin. We had no leads and no suspects for his murder, but we had convincing direct evidence against Sierra for the murders of Lucille Stone and Cameron Whittaker.

Our case was solid. What could possibly go wrong?

The Hall of Justice was home to the offices of the DA and the ME, as well as to the county jail and the superior court of the Criminal Division. For his security and ours, Sierra was being housed and tried right here.

Rich, Cindy, Yuki, and I sat together in the back row of a blond-wood-paneled courtroom that was packed with reporters, the friends and families of Sierra's victims, and a smattering of law students who were able to get in to see the trial of the decade.

At 9:00 a.m. Sierra was brought in through the rear door of Courtroom 2C. A collective gasp nearly sucked up all the air in the room.

The King had cleaned up since I'd last seen him. He'd had

a nice close shave and a haircut. The orange jumpsuit had been swapped out for a gray sports jacket, a freshly pressed pair of slacks, a blue shirt, and a paisley tie. He looked like a fine citizen, except for the ten pounds of shackles around his ankles and wrists that were linked to the belt cinched around his waist.

He clanked over to the defense table. Two marshals removed the handcuffs and took their seats in the first row behind the rail, directly behind Sierra and his attorney, J. C. Fuentes.

Sierra spoke into his lawyer's ear, and Fuentes shook his head furiously, looking very much like a wild animal.

At the prosecution counsel table across the aisle, Red Dog Parisi and two of his ADAs represented the side of good against evil. Parisi was too big to be a snappy dresser, but his navy-blue suit and striped tie gave him a buttoned-up look and set off his coarse auburn hair.

He looked formidable. He looked loaded for bear.

I was sure of it. Kingfisher had met his match. And my money was on Red Dog.

# CHAPTER 20

**THE BUTTERFLIES IN MY** stomach rose up and took a few laps as the Honorable Baron Crispin entered the courtroom and the bailiff asked us all to rise.

Judge Crispin came from Harvard Law, and it was said that he was a viable candidate for the US Supreme Court. I knew him to be a no-nonsense judge, strictly by the book. When he was seated, he took a look at his laptop, exchanged a few words with the court reporter, and then called the court to order.

The judge said a few words about proper decorum and instructed the spectators in what was unacceptable in his court. "This is not reality TV. There will be no outcries or applause. Cell phones must be turned off. If a phone rings, the owner of that phone will be removed from the courtroom. And please, wait for recesses before leaving for any reason. If someone sneezes, let's just *imagine* that others are saying 'God bless you.'"

While the judge was speaking, I was looking at the back of Kingfisher's head. Without warning, the King shot to his feet.

His attorney put a hand on his arm and made a futile attempt to force him back down.

But Kingfisher would not be stopped.

He turned his head toward DA Parisi and shouted, "You are going to die a terrible death if this trial proceeds, Mr. Dog. You, too, Judge Crispy. That's a threat and a promise. A death sentence, too."

Judge Crispin yelled to the marshals, "Get him out of here."

Parisi's voice boomed over the screams and general pandemonium. "Your Honor. Please sequester the jury."

By then the marshals had charged through the gate, kicked chairs out of their way, and cuffed Sierra's wrists, after which they shoved and pushed the defendant across the well and out the rear door.

I was also on my feet, following the marshals and their prisoner out that back door that connected to the private corridor and elevators for court officers and staff.

Attorney J. C. Fuentes was at my heels.

The door closed behind us and Sierra saw me. He said, "You, too, will die, Sergeant Boxer. You are still on my list. I haven't forgotten you."

I shouted at Sierra's guards, "Don't let him talk to anyone. *Anyone.* Do you understand?"

I was panting from fear and stress, but I stayed right on them as they marched Sierra along the section of hallway to the elevators, keeping distance between Sierra and his lawyer. When

Sierra and his guards had gotten inside the elevator, the doors had closed, and the needle on the dial was moving up, I turned on Fuentes.

"Remove yourself from this case."

"You must be kidding."

"I'm dead serious. Tell Crispin that Sierra threatened your life and he will believe you. Or how does this sound? I'll arrest you on suspicion of conspiring to murder Barry Schein. I may do it anyway."

"You don't have to threaten me. I'll be glad to get away from him. Far away."

"You're welcome," I said. "Let's go talk to the judge."

# CHAPTER 21

**CHIEF OF POLICE WARREN** Jacobi's corner office was on the fifth floor of the Hall, overlooking Bryant.

Jacobi and I had once been partners, and over the ten years we had worked together, we had bonded for life. The gunshot injuries he'd gotten on the job had aged him, and he looked ten years older than his fifty-five years.

At present his office was packed to standing room only.

Brady and Parisi, Conklin and I, and every inspector in Homicide, Narcotics, and Robbery were standing shoulder to shoulder as the Kingfisher situation was discussed and assignments were handed out.

There was a firm knock on the door and Mayor Robert Caputo walked in. He nodded at us in a general greeting and asked the chief for a briefing.

Jacobi said, "The jury is sequestered inside the jail. We're organizing additional security details now."

"Inside the actual jail?" said Caputo.

"We have an empty pod of cells on six," Jacobi said of the

vacancy left when a section of the women's jail was relocated to the new jail on 7th Street. He described the plan to bring in mattresses and personal items, all of this calculated to keep the jury free of exposure to media or accidental information leaks.

"We've set up a command center in the lobby, and anything that comes into or out of the sixth floor will go through metal detectors and be visually inspected."

Jacobi explained that the judge had refused to be locked down but that he had 24/7 security at his home. Caputo thanked Jacobi and left the room. When the meeting ended, Brady took me aside.

"Boxer, I'm putting two cars on your house. We need to know where you are at all times. Don't go rogue, okay?"

"Right, Brady. But—"

"Don't tell me you can take care of yourself. Be smart."

Conklin and I took the first shift on the sixth floor, and I made phone calls.

When I got home that evening, I told my protection detail to wait for me.

I took my warm and sleepy Julie out of her bed and filled Mrs. Rose in on my plan as we gathered toys and a traveling bag. When my bodyguards gave me the all clear, I went back downstairs with my still-sleepy baby in my arms. Mrs. Rose and I strapped her into her car seat in the back. Martha jumped in after us.

Deputy sheriffs took over for our beat cops and escorted me

on the long drive to Half Moon Bay. I waited for their okay, and then I parked in my sister's driveway.

I let Martha out and gently extricated my little girl from the car seat. I hugged her awake. She put her hands in my hair and smiled.

"Mommy?"

"Yes, my sweets. Did you have a good nap?"

Catherine came out to meet me. She put her arm around me and walked me and Julie inside her lovely, beachy house near the bay. She had already set up her girls' old crib, and we tried to put a good spin on this dislocation for Julie, but Julie wasn't buying it. She could and did go from smiles to stratospheric protests when she was unhappy.

I didn't want to leave her, either.

I turned to Cat and said, "I've texted Joe. He's on call for whenever you need him. He'll sleep on the couch."

"Sounds good," she said. "I like having a man around the house. Especially one with a gun."

"Don't worry," Cat and I said in unison.

We laughed, hugged, kissed, and then I shushed Julie and told Martha that she was in charge.

I had my hand on my gun when I left Cat's house and got into my car. I stayed in radio contact with my escorts, and with one car in the lead and the other behind me, we started back up the coast to my apartment on Lake Street.

I gripped the wheel so hard my hands hurt, which was preferable to feeling them shake. I stared out at the taillights in front of me. They looked like the malevolent red eyes of those monsters you see in horror movies. Kingfisher was worse than all of them put together.

I hated being afraid of him.

I hated that son of a bitch entirely.

## CHAPTER 22

**AN HOUR AFTER I** got home to my dark and empty apartment, Joe's name lit up the caller ID.

I thumbed the On button, nearly shouting, "What's wrong?"

"Linds, I've got information for you," he said.

"Where are you?"

"On 280 South. Cat called me. Julie is inconsolable. I know I agreed that it was safe to take her there, but honestly, don't you think it would have made more sense for me to come over and stay with the two of you on Lake Street?"

I was filled with complex and contradictory rage.

It was true that it would have been easier, more expeditious, for Joe to have checked into our apartment, slept on our sofa instead of Cat's. True that along with my security detail, we would have been safe right here.

But I wasn't ready for Joe to move back in for a few nights— or whatever. Because along with my justifiable rage, I still loved a man I no longer completely trusted.

"I had to make a quick decision, Joe," I snapped. "What's the information?"

"Reliable sources say that there's Mexican gang activity on the move in San Francisco."

"Could you be more specific?"

"Hey. Blondie. Could you please take it easy?"

"Okay. Sorry," I said. The line was silent. I said, "Joe. Are you still there?"

"I'm sorry, too. I don't like anything about this guy. I've heard that Mala Sangre 'killer elites' have come to town to deliver on Kingfisher's threats. Los Toros activity has also been noted."

"Gang war?"

"I've told you all I know."

"Thanks, Joe. Drive safe. Call me if Julie doesn't settle down."

"Copy that," said Joe. "Be careful."

And the line went dead.

I stood with the phone pressed against my chest for a good long while. Then I called Jacobi.

## CHAPTER 23

**I WATCHED FROM THE** top of the steps up to the Hall the next morning as hundreds of people came to work, lined up to go through the metal detectors, and walked across the garnet-marbled lobby to the elevator banks.

They all looked worried.

That was both unusual and understandable. Kingfisher's presence on the seventh floor felt like a kryptonite meteor had dropped through the roof and was lodged in the jail. He was draining the energy from everyone who worked here.

I went inside, passed through metal detection, and then took the stairs to the squad room.

Brady had called a special early-morning meeting because of the intel from Joe. He stood at the head of the open-space bull pen, his back to the door, the muted TV hanging above his head.

Cops from all departments—the night shift, the swing shift, and our shift—were perched on the edges of desks, leaned against walls. There were even some I didn't recognize from the northern station crammed into the room. I saw deputy sheriffs, motorcycle cops, and men and women in plain clothes and blue.

Brady said, "I've called y'all together because we could be looking at a citywide emergency situation."

He spoke about the possibility of drug gang warfare and he answered questions about Mala Sangre, about Kingfisher, about cops who had been killed at the King's order. They asked about the upcoming rescheduled trial and about practical issues. The duty rosters. The chain of command.

Brady was honest and direct to a fault. I didn't get a sense that the answers he gave were satisfying. But honestly, he had no idea what to expect.

When the meeting was over, when the dozen of us on the day shift were alone with our lieutenant, he said, "The jurors are having fits. They don't know what's going on, but they can see out the windows. They see a lot of cops.

"The mayor's coming over to talk to them."

The mayor was a great people handler.

I was in the sixth-floor dayroom when Mayor Caputo visited the jurors and explained that they were carrying out their civic duty. "It's not just that this is important," he said. "This could be the most important work of your entire lives."

That afternoon one of the jurors had a heart attack and was evacuated. A second juror, a primary caregiver for a dependent parent, was excused. Alternates, who were also in our emergency jury lockup, moved up to full jurors.

When I was getting ready to leave after my twelve-hour day, Brady told me that an ambitious defender, Jake Penney, had spent the last four days with Jorge Sierra and had said that he was good to go.

The countdown to Sierra's trial had begun again.

# CHAPTER 24

**I WAS SLEEPING WHEN** Joe called.

The time on my phone was midnight, eight hours before the trial was to begin.

"What's wrong?" I asked.

"Julie's fine. The SFPD website is down. The power is out at the Hall."

I turned on the TV news and saw mayhem on Bryant Street. Barricades had been set up. Reporters and cameramen shouted questions at uniformed officers. The Hall of Justice was so dark it looked like an immense mausoleum.

I nuked instant coffee and sat cross-legged in Joe's chair, watching the tube. At 1:00 a.m. fire could be seen leaping at the glass doors that faced the intersection of Bryant and Boardman Place.

A network reporter said to the camera, "Chet, I'm hearing that there was an explosion inside the lobby."

I couldn't take this anymore. I texted Brady. He was rushed. He typed, *Security is checking in with me up and down the line. Don't come in, Boxer.*

Then, as suddenly as they had gone out, the lights in the Hall came back on.

My laptop was on the coffee table and I switched it on. I punched in the address for the SFPD site, and I was watching when a title appeared on our own front page: *This was a test.*

It was signed *Mala Sangre.*

Kingfisher's cartel.

This had been their test for what? For shutting down our video surveillance? For sending out threatening messages? For disabling our electronic locks inside the jail? For smuggling bombs into the Hall?

It would have been a laughable threat if Kingfisher hadn't killed two people from the confines of his windowless cell. How had he pulled that off? What else could he do?

I called Cat. She said, "Lindsay, she's fine. She was in sleepy land when the phone rang."

I heard Julie crying and Joe's voice in the background saying, "Julie-Bug, I'm here."

"Sorry. Sorry," I said. "I'll call you in the morning. Thanks for everything, Cat."

I called Jacobi. His voice was steady. I liked that.

"I was just going to call you," he said. "The bomb was stuck under the lip of the sign-in desk. It was small, but if it had gone off during the daytime…" After a pause Jacobi began again. "Hounds and the bomb squad are going through the building. The trial is postponed until further notice."

"Good," I said. But I didn't feel good. It felt like anything could happen. That Kingfisher was in charge of it all.

My intercom buzzed. It was half past one.

Cerrutti, my designated security guard, said, "Sergeant, Dr. Washburn is here."

Tears of relief filled my eyes and no one had to see them. I buzzed my friend in.

# CHAPTER 25

**CLAIRE CAME THROUGH MY** door bringing hope, love, warmth, and the scent of tea roses. All good things.

She said, "I have to crash here, Lindsay. I drove to the office. It's closed off from both the street and the back door to the Hall. It's too late to drive all the way home."

I hugged her. I needed that hug and I thought she did, too. I pointed her to Joe's big chair, with the best view of the TV. On-screen now, a live report from Bryant Street.

Wind whipped through the reporter's hair, turning her scarf into a pennant, making her microphone crackle.

She squinted at the camera and said, "I've just gotten off the phone with the mayor's office and can confirm reports that there are no fatalities from the bomb. The prisoner, Jorge Sierra, also known as Kingfisher, remains locked in his cell.

"The mayor has also confirmed that Sierra's trial has been postponed until the Hall is cleared. If you work at 850 Bryant, please check our website to see if your office is open."

When the segment ended, Claire talked to me about the

chaos outside the Hall. She couldn't get to her computer and she needed to reach her staff.

Yuki called at two. "You're watching?"

"Yes. Is Brady with you?"

"No," she said. "But three cruisers are outside our apartment building. And I have a gun. Nothing like this has ever happened around a trial in San Francisco. Protesters? Yes. Bombs? No."

I asked her, "Do you know Kingfisher's new attorney?"

"Jake Penney. I don't know him. But this I do know. He's got balls."

Claire made soup from leftovers and defrosted a pound cake. I unscrewed a bottle of chilled cheap Chardonnay. Claire took off her shoes and reclined in the chair. I gave her a pair of socks and we settled into half a night of TV together.

I must have slept for a few minutes, because I woke to my cell phone buzzing on the floor beside the sofa.

Who was it now? Joe? Cat? Jacobi?

"Sergeant Boxer, it's Elena."

It took me a moment to put a face to a name. It came to me. Elena, a.k.a. Maura Steele, was Jorge Sierra's reluctant wife.

I bolted into an upright position. Had we thought to protect her? *No.*

"Are you okay?"

"I'm fine. I have an idea."

"I'm listening," I said.

# CHAPTER 26

**WHEN I'D MET WITH** Elena Sierra, she had let me know that she wanted nothing to do with her husband. I had given her my card but never expected to hear from her.

What had changed her mind?

I listened hard as she laid out her plan. It was brilliant and simple. I had made this *same* offer to Sierra and utterly failed to close the deal. But Kingfisher didn't love *me*.

Now I had reason to hope that Elena could help put this nightmare to bed.

The meeting between Elena and her husband was arranged quickly. By late afternoon the next day our cameras were rolling upstairs in a barred room reserved for prisoners and their attorneys.

Elena wore a belted vibrant-purple sweaterdress and designer boots and looked like a cover girl. She sat across the table from Sierra. He wore orange and was chained so that he couldn't stand or move his hands. He looked amused.

I stood in a viewing room with Conklin and Brady, watching live video of Elena's meeting with Sierra, and heard him suggest several things he would like to do with her. It was creepy, but she cut him off by saying, "I'm not here for your pleasure, Jorge. I'm trying to help you."

Sierra leaned forward and said, "You don't want to help me. You want only money and power. How do I know? Because I created you."

"Jorge. We only have a few more minutes. I'm offering you the chance to see your children—"

"Mine? I'm not so sure."

"All you have to do is to plead guilty."

"That's all? Whose payroll are you on, Elena? Who are you working for, bitch whore?"

Elena got to her feet and slapped her husband hard across the face.

Joy surged through my body. I could almost feel my right palm stinging as if I had slapped him myself.

The King laughed at his wife, then turned his head and called out through the bars, "Take me back."

Two guards appeared at the cage door and the King was led out. When he was gone, Elena looked at the camera and shrugged. She looked embarrassed. She said, "I lost my temper."

I pressed the intercom. "You did fine. Thank you, Elena."

"Well, that was edifying," said Brady.

"She tried," I said to Brady. "I don't see what else she could have done."

I turned to Rich and said, "Let's drive her home."

# CHAPTER 27

**ELENA SIERRA HAD CURLED** up in the backseat and leaned against the window. "He's subhuman," she said. "My father warned me, but I was eighteen. He was…I don't remember what the hell I was thinking. *If* I was thinking."

There was a long pause, as if she was trying to remember when she had fallen in love with Kingfisher.

"I'm coming to the trial," Elena said. "I want to see his face when he's found guilty. My father wants to be there, too."

Then she stared silently out the window until we pulled up to her deluxe apartment building on California Street. Conklin walked Elena into the lobby, and when he came back to the car, I was behind the wheel.

I switched on the car radio, which broke into a cacophony of bleats and static. I gave dispatch our coordinates as we left Nob Hill and said that we were heading back to the Hall.

At just about half past six we were on Race Street. We'd been stuck behind a FedEx truck for several blocks, until now, when it ran a yellow light, leaving us flat-footed at the red.

I cursed and the gray sedan behind us pulled out into the oncoming lane, its wheels jerking hard to the right, and the driver braked at an angle twenty-five feet ahead of our left front bumper.

I shouted, "What the hell?"

But by the time the word *hell* was out of my mouth, Conklin had his door open and was yelling to me, *"Out of the car. With me."*

I got it.

I snapped mental images as four men burst from the gray sedan into our headlight beams. One wore a black knit cap and bulky jacket. Another had a gold grille plating his teeth. The one coming out of the driver's side was holding an AK. One with a black scarf over half his face ducked out of view.

I dropped below the dash and pulled myself out the passenger side, slid down to the street. Conklin and I hunched behind the right front wheel, using the front of the car as a shield. We were both carrying large, high-capacity semiautomatics, uncomfortable as hell to wear, but my God, I was glad we had them.

A fusillade of bullets punched holes through the door that had been to my left just seconds before. Glass crazed and shattered.

I poked my head up during a pause in oncoming gunfire, and using the hood as a gun brace, Conklin and I let loose with a fury of return fire.

In that moment I saw the one with the AK drop his weapon. His gun or his hand had been hit, or the gun had slipped out of his grasp. When the shooter bent to retrieve it, Conklin and I fired and kept firing until the bastard was down.

For an eternal minute and a half curses flew, and shots punctured steel, exploded the shop windows behind us, and smacked into the front end of our car. If these men worked for the King, they could not let us get away.

Conklin and I alternately rose from behind the car just enough to brace our guns and return fire, ducking as our attackers unloaded on us with the fury of hell.

We reloaded and kept shooting. My partner took out the guy with the glittering teeth, and I wasn't sure, but I might have winged the one with the scarf.

The light turned green.

Traffic resumed, and while some vehicles streamed past, others balked, blocking cars behind them, leaving them in the line of fire.

There was a lull in the shooting, and when I peeked above our car, I saw the driver of the gray Ford backing up, turning the wheel into traffic, gunning the engine, then careening across the intersection at N17th.

I took a stance and emptied my Glock into the rear of the Ford, hoping to hit the gas tank. A tire blew, but the car kept going. I looked down at the two dead men in the street as Conklin kicked their guns away and looked for ID.

I got into the car, grabbed the mic, shouted my badge number, and reported to dispatch.

"Shots fired. Two men down. Send patrol cars and a bus to Race and N17th. BOLO for a gray Ford four-door with shot-out windows and flat right rear tire heading east on Race at high speed. Nevada plates, partial number Whiskey Four Niner."

Within minutes the empty, shot-riddled Ford was found ditched a few blocks away on 17th Street. Conklin and I sat for a while in our shot-to-shit squad car, listening to the radio snap, crackle, and pop while waiting for a ride back to the Hall. My right hand was numb and the aftershock of my gun's recoil still resonated through my bones.

I was glad to feel it.

I said to Richie, as if he didn't already know, "We're damned lucky to be alive."

# CHAPTER 28

**TWO HOURS AFTER THE** shoot-out Conklin and I learned that the Ford had been stolen. The guns were untraceable. The only ID found on the two dead men were their Mala Sangre tats. Had to be that Kingfisher's men had been following us or following Elena.

We turned in our guns and went directly down the street to McBain's, a cross between a place where everyone knows your name and the *Star Wars* cantina. It was fully packed now with cops, lawyers, bail bondsmen, and a variety of clerks and administrators. The ball game was blaring loudly on the tube, competing with some old tune coming from the ancient Wurlitzer in the back.

Rich and I found two seats at the bar, ordered beer, toasted the portrait of Captain McBain hanging over the backbar, and proceeded to drink. We had to process the bloodcurdling firefight and there was no better place than here.

Conklin sat beside me shaking his head, probably having thoughts like my own, which were so vivid that I could still hear the *rat-a-tat-tat* of lead punching through steel and see the faces of the bangers we'd just "put down like dogs." I stank of gunpowder and fear.

We were alive not just because of what we knew about bad guys with guns, or because Conklin and I worked so well together that we were like two halves of a whole.

That had contributed to it, but mostly, we were alive and drinking because of the guy who'd dropped his AK and given us a two-second advantage.

After I'd downed half of my second beer, I told Conklin, "We weren't wearing vests, for Christ's sake. This is so unfair to Julie."

"Cut it out," he said. "Don't make me say she's lucky to have you as a mom."

"Fine."

"Two dirtbags are dead," he said. "We did that. We won't feel bad about that."

"That guy with the AK."

"He's in hell," said Rich, "kicking his own ass."

Oates, the bartender, asked if I was ready for another, but I shook my head and covered the top of my glass. Just then I felt an arm go around my shoulders. I started. It was Brady behind us, all white blond and blue-eyed, and he had an arm around Conklin, too.

He gave my shoulder a squeeze, his way of saying, *Thanks. You did good. I'm proud of you.*

"Come back to the house," Brady said. "I've got your new weapons and rides home for both of y'all."

"I've only had one beer," Rich lied.

"I've got rides home for *both* of y'all," Brady repeated.

He put some bills down on the bar. Malcolm, the tipsy dude on my left, pointed to the dregs of my beer and asked, "You done with that, Lindsay?"

I passed him my glass.

It was ten fifteen when I got to Cat's. I took a scalding shower, washed my hair, and buffed myself dry. Martha sat with her head in my lap while I ate chicken and noodles à la Gloria Rose. I was scraping the plate when the phone rang.

"I heard about what happened today," Joe said.

"Yeah. It was over so fast. In two minutes I'd pulled my gun and there were men lying dead in the street."

"Good result. Are you okay?"

"Never better," I said, sounding a little hysterical to my own ears. I'm sure Joe heard it, too.

"Okay. Good. Do you need anything?"

"No, but thanks. Thanks for calling."

I slept with Martha and Julie that night, one arm around each of my girls. I slept hard and I dreamed hard and I was still holding on to Julie when she woke me up in the morning.

I blinked away the dream fragments and remembered that Kingfisher would be facing the judge and jury today.

I had to move fast so that I wasn't late to court.

# CHAPTER 29

**CONKLIN AND I WERE** at our desks at eight, filling out the incident report and watching the time.

Kingfisher's trial was due to start at nine, but would the trial actually begin? I thought about the power outage that had occurred two days ago, followed by the bomb explosion and the threatening message that had read *This was a test. Mala Sangre.* And I wondered if Kingfisher had already left the Hall through the drain in his shower, El Chapo style.

His trial had been postponed three times so far, but I had dressed for court nonetheless. I was wearing my good charcoal-gray pants, my V-neck silk sweater under a Ralph Lauren blazer, and my flat-heeled Cole Haan shoes. My hair gleamed and I'd even put on lipstick. *That's for you, Mr. Kingfisher.*

Conklin had just dunked his empty coffee container into the trash can when Len Parisi's name lit up on my console.

I said to Conklin, "What now?" and grabbed the phone.

Parisi said, "Boxer, you and Conklin got a second?"

"Sure. What's up?"

"Counsel for the defense is in my office."

"Be right there." I hung up, then said to Conklin, "I'm guessing Sierra wants to change his plea to insanity."

He said, "From your lips to God's ears."

It was a grim thought. In the unlikely event that Kingfisher could be found guilty because of mental disease or defect, he would be institutionalized and one day might be set free.

"There's just no way," said Conklin.

"Wanna bet?"

Conklin dug into his wallet and tossed a single onto the desk. I topped his dollar bill with one of mine and weighed down our bet with a stapler.

Then we booked it down the stairs and along the second-floor corridor at a good pace, before entering the maze of cubicles outside the DA's office. Parisi's office door was open. He signaled for us to come in.

Jake Penney, the King's new attorney, sat in the chair beside Parisi's oversized desk. He was about thirty-five and was good-looking in a flawless, *The Bachelor* kind of way. Because Cindy reearched him and reported back, I knew he was on the fast track at a topflight law firm.

Kingfisher had hired one of the best.

Conklin and I took the sofa opposite Parisi, and Penney angled his chair toward us.

He said, "I want to ask my client to take Elena's offer. He changes his plea to guilty, and he goes to a maximum-security prison within a few hours' drive of his wife's residence. That's win-win. Saves the people the cost of a trial. Keeps Mr. Sierra in the USA with no death penalty and a chance to see his kids every now and again. It's worth another try."

Parisi said to Conklin and me, "I'm okay with this, but I wanted to run it by you before I gave Mr. Penney an okay to offer this deal to Sierra."

I said, "You'll be in the room with them, Len?"

"Absolutely."

"Mr. Penney should go through metal detection and agree to be patted down before and after his meeting."

"Okay, Mr. Penney?"

"Of course."

There was a clock on the wall, the face a hand-drawn illustration of a red bulldog.

The time was 8:21.

If the King's attorney could make a deal for his client, it had to be now or never.

# CHAPTER 30

**CONKLIN AND I WAITED** in Parisi's office as the second hand swiped the bulldog's face and time whizzed around the dial.

What was taking so long? Deal? Or no deal?

I was ready to go up to the seventh floor and crash the conference when Parisi and Penney came through the door.

"He wouldn't buy it," Parisi said. He went to his closet and took out his blue suit jacket.

Penney said, "He maintains his innocence. He wants to walk out of court a free man."

It took massive willpower for me not to roll my eyes and shout, *Yeah, right. Of course he's innocent!*

Parisi shrugged into his jacket, tightened the knot in his tie, glanced at the clock. Then he said, "I told Sierra about the attack on you two by Mala Sangre thugs. I said that if the violence stops now, and if he is convicted, I will arrange for him to do his time at the prison of his choice, Pelican Bay. He said, 'Okay. I agree. No more violence.' We shook on it. For whatever that's worth."

Pelican Bay was a supermax-security prison in Del Norte

County, at the very northwest tip of California, about fifteen miles south of the Oregon border. It was a good six-and-a-half-hour drive from here. The prison population was made up of the state's most violent criminals and rated number one for most gangs and murders inside its walls. The King would feel right at home there.

"I'll see you in court," Parisi said to Penney.

The two men shook hands. Conklin and I wished Parisi luck, then headed down to the courtroom.

Kingfisher had agreed to the safety of all involved in his trial, but entering Courtroom 2C, I felt as frightened as I had when I woke up this morning with a nightmare in my mind.

An AK had chattered in the King's hands.

And then he'd gotten me.

# CHAPTER 31

**KINGFISHER'S DAY IN COURT** had dawned again.

All stood when Judge Crispin, looking irritated from his virtual house arrest, took the bench. The gallery sat down with a collective *whoosh,* and the judge delivered his rules of decorum to a new set of spectators. No one could doubt him when he said, "Outbursts will be dealt with by immediate removal from this courtroom."

I sat in a middle row between two strangers. Richie was seated a few rows ahead to my right. Elena Sierra sat behind the defense table, where she had a good view of the back of her husband's head. A white-haired man sat beside her and whispered to her. He had to be her father.

The jurors entered the box and were sworn in.

There were five women and nine men, including the remaining alternates. It was a diverse group in age and ethnicity. I saw a range of emotion in their faces: stolid fury, relief, curiosity, and a high level of excitement.

I felt all those emotions, too.

During the judge's address to the jurors every one of them took a long look at the defendant. In fact, it was hard to look away from Kingfisher. The last time he was at the defense table, he'd cleaned up and appeared almost respectable. Today the King was patchily shaven and had flecks of blood on his collar. He seemed dazed and subdued.

To my eye, he looked as though he'd used up all his tricks and couldn't believe he was actually on trial. By contrast, his attorney, Jake Penney, wore his pin-striped suit with aplomb. DA Leonard Parisi looked indomitable.

All stood to recite the Pledge of Allegiance, and then there was a prolonged rustle as seats were retaken. Someone coughed. A cell phone clattered to the floor. Conklin turned his head and we exchanged looks.

Kingfisher had threatened us since the nasty Finders Keepers case last year—and *still* he haunted my dreams. Would the jury find him guilty of killing Stone and Whittaker? Would this monstrous killer spend the rest of his life inside the high, razor-wired walls of Pelican Bay State Prison?

The bailiff called the court to order, and Judge Crispin asked Len Parisi if he was ready to present his case.

I felt pride in the big man as he walked out into the well. I could almost feel the floor shake. He welcomed the jury and thanked them for bearing down under unusually trying conditions in the interest of justice.

Then he launched into his opening statement.

# CHAPTER 32

**I'D NEVER BEFORE SEEN** Len Parisi present a case to a jury. He was an intimidating man and a powerful one. As district attorney, he was responsible for investigating and prosecuting crime in this city and was at the head of three divisions: Operations, Victims Services, and Special Operations.

But he was never more impressive than he was today, standing in for our murdered friend and colleague, ADA Barry Schein.

Parisi held the jury's attention with his presence and his intensity, and then he spoke.

"Ladies and Gentlemen, the defendant, Jorge Sierra, is a merciless killer. In the course of this trial you will hear witness testimony and see video evidence of the defendant in the act of shooting two innocent women to death."

Parisi paused, but I didn't think it was for effect. It seemed to me that he was inside the crime now, seeing the photos of the victims' bloodied bodies at the Vault. He cleared his throat and began again.

"One of those women was Lucille Stone, twenty-eight years old. She worked in marketing, and for a long time she was one of Mr. Sierra's girlfriends. She was unarmed when she was killed. Never carried a gun, and she had done nothing to Mr. Sierra. But, according to Lucy's friends, she had decisively ended the relationship.

"Cameron Whittaker was Lucy's friend. She was a substitute teacher, volunteered at a food bank, and had nothing whatsoever to do with Mr. Sierra or his associates. She was what is called collateral damage. She was in the wrong place at the wrong time."

I turned my eyes to the jury and they were with Len all the way. He walked along the railing that separated the jury box from the well of the courtroom.

He said, "One minute these friends were enjoying a girls' night out in an upscale nightclub, sitting together at the bar. And the next minute they were shot to death by the defendant, who thought he could get away with murder in full sight of 150 people, some of whom aimed their cell phones and took damning videos of this classic example of premeditated murder.

"I say 'premeditated' because the shooting was conceived before the night in question when Lucy Stone rejected Mr. Sierra's advances. He followed her. He found her. He taunted her and he menaced her. And then he put two bullet holes in her body and even more in the body of her friend.

"Lucy Stone didn't know that when she refused to open her door to him, he immediately planned to enact his revenge—"

Parisi had his hands on the railing when an explosion cracked through the air inside the courtroom.

It was a stunning, deafening blast. I dove for the floor and covered the back of my neck with my hands. Screams followed the report. Chairs scraped back and toppled. I looked up and saw that the bomb had gone off behind me and had blown open the main doors.

Smoke filled the courtroom, obscuring my vision. The spectators panicked. They swarmed forward, away from the blast and toward the judge's bench.

Someone yelled, "Your Honor, can you hear me?"

I heard shots coming from the well; one, then two more.

I was on my feet, but the shots sent the freaked-out spectators in the opposite direction, away from the bench, toward me and through the doors out into the hallway.

Who had fired those shots? The only guns that could have passed through metal detection into the Hall had to belong to law enforcement. Had anyone been hit?

As the room cleared and the smoke lifted, I took stock of the damage. The double main doors were nearly unhinged, but the destruction was slight. The bomb seemed more like a diversion than a forceful explosion meant to kill, maim, or destroy property.

A bailiff helped Parisi to his feet. Judge Crispin pulled himself up from behind the bench, and the jury was led out the side doorway. Conklin headed toward me as the last of the spectators flowed out the main doors and cops ran in.

"EMTs are on the way," he said.

That's when I saw that the defense table, where the King had been sitting with his attorney, had flipped onto its side.

Penney looked around and called out, "Help! I need help here!"

My ears still rang from the blast. I made my way around overturned chairs to where Kingfisher lay on his side in a puddle of blood. He reached out his hand and beckoned to me.

"I'm here," I said. "Talk to me."

The King had been shot. There was a ragged bullet hole in his shoulder, blood pumping from his belly, and more blood pouring from a wound at the back of his head. There were shell casings on the floor.

He was in pain and maybe going into shock, but he was conscious.

His voice sounded like a whisper to my deafened ears. But I read him, loud and clear.

"Elena did this," he said. "Elena, my little Elena."

Then his face relaxed. His hand dropped. His eyes closed and he died.

## CHAPTER 33

**JORGE SIERRA'S FUNERAL WAS** held at a Catholic cemetery in Crescent City, a small northwest California town on the ocean named for the crescent-shaped bay that defined it.

Among the seventy-five hundred people included in the census were the fifteen hundred inmates of nearby Pelican Bay State Prison.

It was either irony or payback, but Elena had picked this spot because her husband had asked to be imprisoned at Pelican Bay and now he would be within eight miles of it—forever.

The graveyard had been virtually abandoned. The ground was flat, bleak, with several old headstones that had been tipped over by vandals or by weather. The chapel needed paint, and just beyond the chapel was a potholed parking lot.

Several black cars, all government property, were parked there, and a dozen FBI agents stood in a loose perimeter around the grave site and beside the chapel within the parking lot with a view of the road.

I was with Conklin and Parisi. My partner and I had been

told that Sierra was dead and buried once before. This time I had looked into the coffin. The King was cold and dead, but I still wanted to see the box go into the ground.

Conklin had suffered along with me when Sierra had terrorized me last year, and even though justice had been cheated, we were both relieved it was over.

The FBI had sent agents to the funeral to see who showed up. The King's murder inside the courthouse was an unsolved mystery. The smoke and the surging crowd had blocked the camera's view of the defense table. Elena Sierra and her father, Pedro Quintana, had been questioned separately within twelve hours of the shooting and had said that they had hit the floor after the blast, eyes down when the bullets were fired. They hadn't seen the shooting.

So they said.

Both had come for Sierra's send-off, and Elena had brought her children to say good-bye to their father.

Elena looked lovely in black. Eight-year-old Javier and six-year-old Alexa bowed their heads as the priest spoke over their father's covered coffin at graveside. The little girl cried.

I studied this tableau.

Elena had many reasons to want her husband dead. But she had no military background, nothing that convinced me that she could lean over the railing and shoot her husband point-blank in the back of the head.

Her father, however, was a different story.

I'd done some research into Mexican gangsters and learned that Pedro Quintana was the retired head of Los Toros, the original gang that had raised and trained Sierra on his path to becoming the mightiest drug kingpin of them all.

Sierra had famously disposed of Quintana after he split off from Los Toros and formed Mala Sangre, the new and more powerful drug and crime cartel.

Both Elena and her father had motive to put Sierra down, but how had one or both of them pulled off this shooting in open court?

I'd called Joe last night to brainstorm with him. Despite the state of our marriage, Joe Molinari had background to spare as an agent in USA clandestine services, as well as from his stint as deputy to the director of Homeland Security.

He theorized that during the power outage in the Hall, a C-4 explosive charge had been slapped onto the hinges of Judge Crispin's courtroom doors. It was plausible that one of the hundreds of law enforcement personnel prowling the Hall that night had been paid to set this charge, and it was possible for a lump of plastic explosive to go unnoticed.

A package containing a small gun, ammo, and a remote-controlled detonator could have been smuggled in at the same time, left where only Sierra's killer could find it. It could even have been passed to the killer or killers the morning of the trial.

Had Elena and her father orchestrated this perfect act of retribution? If so, I thought they were going to get away with it.

These were my thoughts as I stood with Conklin and Parisi in the windswept and barren cemetery watching the lowering of the coffin, Elena throwing flowers into the grave, the first shovel of dirt, her children clinging to their mother's skirt.

The moment ended when a limo pulled around a circular drive and Elena Sierra's family went to it and got inside.

Rich said to me, "I'm going to hitch a ride back with Red Dog. Okay with you?"

I said it was. We hugged good-bye.

Another car, an aging Mercedes, swung around the circle of dead grass and stone. It stopped for me. I opened the back door and reached out to my baby girl in her car seat. She was wearing a pink sweater and matching hat knit for her by her lovely nanny. I gave Julie a big smooch and what we call a huggy-wuffle.

Then I got into the front passenger seat.

Joe was driving.

"Zoo?" he said.

"Zoooooooo," came from behind.

"It's unanimous," I said. "The zoos have it."

Joe put his hand behind my neck and pulled me toward him. I hadn't kissed him in a long time. But I kissed him then.

There'd be plenty of time to talk later.

# EPILOGUE

# CHAPTER 34

**THE LIMO DRIVER WHO** was bringing Elena Sierra and the children back from a shopping trip couldn't park at the entrance to her apartment building. A long-used family car was stopped right in front of the walkway, where an elderly man was helping his wife out of the car with her walker. The doorman ran outside to help the old couple with their cumbersome luggage.

Elena told her driver, "Leave us right here, Harlan. Thanks. See you in the morning."

After opening the doors for herself and her children, Elena took the two shopping bags from her driver, saying, "I've got it. Thanks."

Doors closed with solid thunks, the limo pulled away, and the kids surrounded their mother, asking her for money to buy churros from the ice cream shop down the block at the corner.

She said, "We don't need churros. We have milk and granola cookies." But she finally relented, set down the groceries, found a five-dollar bill in her purse, and gave it to Javier.

"Please get me one, too," she called after her little boy.

Elena picked up her grocery bags, and as she stood up, she saw two men in bulky jackets—one with a black scarf covering the bottom of his face and the other with a knit cap—crossing the street toward her.

She recognized them as Jorge's men and knew without a doubt that they were coming to kill her. Mercifully, the children were running and were now far down the block.

The one with the scarf, Alejandro, aimed his gun at the doorman and fired. The gun had a suppressor, and the sound of the discharge was so soft the old man hadn't heard it, didn't understand what had happened. He tried to attend to the fallen doorman, while Elena said to the soldier wearing the cap, "Not out here. Please."

Invoking what residual status she might have as the King's widow, Elena turned and walked into the modern, beautifully appointed lobby, her back prickling with expectation of a bullet to her spine.

She walked past the young couple sitting on a love seat, past the young man leashing his dog, and pressed the elevator button. The doors instantly slid open and the two men followed her inside.

The doors closed.

Elena stood at the rear with one armed man standing to her left and the other to her right. She looked straight ahead, thinking about the next few minutes as the elevator rose upward, then chimed as it opened directly into her living room.

Esteban, the shooter with the knit cap, had the words *Mala*

*Sangre* inked on the side of his neck. He stepped ahead of her into the room, looked around at the antiques, the books, the art on the walls. He went to the plate-glass window overlooking the Transamerica Pyramid and the great bay.

"Nice view, Mrs. Sierra," he said with a booming voice. "Maybe you'd like to be looking out the window now. That would be easiest."

"Don't hurt my children," she said. "They are Jorge's. His blood."

She went to the window and placed her hands on the glass. She heard a door open inside the apartment. A familiar voice said loudly, "Drop your guns. Do it now."

Alejandro whipped around, but before he could fire, Elena's father cut him down with a shot to the throat, two more to the chest as he fell.

Pedro Quintana said to the man with the cap, who was holding his hands above his head, "Esteban, get down on your knees while I am deciding what to do with you."

Esteban obeyed, dropping to his knees, keeping his hands up while facing Elena's father, and beseeching him in Spanish.

"Pedro, please. I have known you for twenty years. I named my oldest son for you. I was loyal, but Jorge, he threatened my family. I can prove myself. Elena, I'm sorry. *Por favor.*"

Elena walked around the dead man, who was bleeding on her fine Persian carpet where her children liked to play, and took the gun from her father's hand.

She aimed at Esteban and fired into his chest. He fell sideways, grabbed at his wound, and grunted, *"Dios."*

Elena shot him three more times.

When her husband's soldiers were dead, Elena made calls: First to Harlan to pick up the children immediately and keep them in the car. "Papa will meet you on the corner in five minutes. Wait for him. Take directions from him."

Then she called the police and told them that she had shot two intruders who had attempted to murder her.

Her father stretched out his arms and Elena went in for a hug. Her father said, "Finish what we started. It's yours now, Elena."

"Thank you, Papa."

She went to the bar and poured out two drinks, gave one glass to her father.

They toasted. "Viva Los Toros."

Their cartel would be at the top again.

This was the way it was always meant to be.

## CHAPTER 35

**EMERGING FROM THE ELEVATOR** that opened into the apartment, I switched on my body cam. I wasn't sure what to expect from Elena and her father at the scene of a triple homicide, but I knew enough about the Toros—or should I say the Mala Sangres—by now to make sure I got it on the record.

I couldn't have imagined a more opulent locale for a murder. It was a tomb with a view for Mr. Esteban. Dr. Claire Washburn, my dear friend, standing over the bodies, was framed by the panoramic city vista.

"Hello, Inspector Boxer," Elena said as she approached, looking as glamorous as anyone could in the midst of a gruesome crime scene. Her father stood near a chrome-topped bar cart in the corner, already deep into a glass of something that made me jealous from twenty feet.

"I see you've got some fresh corpses on your hands," I said.

Elena glanced over her elegant shoulder at her father, then turned back to me. "Come with me to the kitchen, Inspector Boxer. The smell of blood is making me sick. Unless you'd like a drink first?" She paused for her captive audience, then flashed a chilling smile my way. "Word has it that you prefer to drink your calories."

"No, thank you." I went along with her ploy, following her into the sleek kitchen. Here was my chance to see the latest in high-end appliances. My own home upgrade was never going to happen, not as long as criminals like Elena and her Toros were running the streets.

"Inspector Boxer, you will of course have heard about the attempted attack on my family this afternoon," she said as soon as we were alone. "It's been a difficult day. Why are you here? Won't the examiner's report suffice, or could you not resist another opportunity to harass us?"

I couldn't let her get away with playing the victim, not now, with three bodies cooling under her feet. "These stiffs can't be scored to Kingfisher's kill list. Does today mark the first entry on yours, or am I not giving you enough credit?"

"Must you taunt, Inspector Boxer? I've just buried Jorge," she said, bearing zero resemblance to a grieving widow. "I truly regret not knowing my husband better," she went on, looking into my eyes as if I were her confessor. "Not understanding how his mind worked. But you did."

There was no hiding my hand in either of his deaths, the false or the all-too-real one. And now here I was, face-to-face with his beloved assassin—and my cunning adversary.

"You took him down, didn't you? And then you convinced

me to help you seal his fate all over again," she said. "I want to know how you did it, every last detail."

"My history with your husband is the last thing you should be worried about right now, Mrs. Sierra. Once you're arrested on this murder charge, who is going to look after Javier and Alexa?" I asked bluntly. "They're too young to run the family business on their own."

"I want you to leave my father out of this. He's still recovering from the shock of seeing my late husband gunned down in the courtroom."

"Committing a murder can be even more traumatic than witnessing one, wouldn't you agree, Mrs. Sierra?"

I might have detected a slight shake of the head, but then she shifted gears.

"Mother to mother," Elena said, "you should be grateful to me that Esteban is gone. He was the one closing in on Julie in the days leading up to the trial. You know as well as I do that she could have been shot, or worse."

There it was, the lowest of blows. She was beginning to enjoy herself, challenging me to feel her power. I leaned into the curve.

"What do you mean, 'grateful'?"

Ever the polite hostess, she covered her mouth before laughing in my face. "The city has never been cleaner. The SFPD wouldn't dare bring me in," she said. "And you won't let them."

"We're going to be spending a lot of time together while I find out exactly what happened here today," I promised.

Elena said, "Neither one of us is stupid. I don't do drugs. I don't even like hearing about drugs. But we're intelligent women, you and I, and we have to live in the world. We'd be fooling ourselves if we pretended businesses like my family's would just disappear because drugs don't fit into our view of the world our children should live in. I'm a realist, a diplomat. If the world is what it is, let it at least be managed in a civilized way." She smiled that chilling smile again. "Of course I would never hurt your daughter—that I promise. Now if you want to arrest me in my own home, go right ahead."

I stared at Elena for a long moment. Then I turned and walked away from her, toward the elevator, toward the streets I knew she owned.

"Where are you going, Inspector Boxer?"

"Home. To be with my little girl."

**Can a little black dress change everything?**

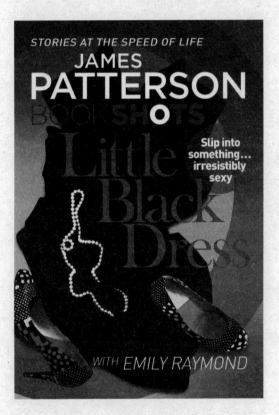

**Read on for an extract**

**I SPOTTED IT ON** the Bergdorf sale rack: see-through black chiffon layered over a simple black sheath, cut to skim lightly over the hips and fall just above the knee. Paired with a thin gold belt, there was something Grecian, even goddessy, about it.

It was somehow subtle yet spectacular. Not a dress, but a *Dress*.

When I tried it on, I was no longer Jane Avery, age thirty-five, overworked editor at Manhattan's *Metropolitan* magazine and recent divorcée. I was Jane Avery, age none of your business, a card-carrying member of the media elite, a woman who was single and proud of it.

Even at 40 percent off, the Dress was a minor fortune. I decided to buy it anyway.

And that purchase changed everything.

**IN THE OPULENT LIMESTONE** lobby of the Four Seasons New York, I handed over my Amex. "A city-view king, please." No tremor in my voice at all. Nothing to betray the pounding of my heart, the adrenaline flooding my veins.

*Am I really about to do this?*

*Maybe I should have had another glass of rosé.*

The desk clerk tapped quickly on her keyboard. "We have a room on the fortieth floor," she said. "Where are you two visiting from?"

I shot a glance over my shoulder. *Honestly? About twenty-five blocks from here.* My knees were turning into Jell-O.

Behind me, Michael Bishop, a thumb hooked in the belt loop of his jeans, flashed his gorgeous smile—first at me, then at the clerk. "Ohio, miss," he said, giving his muscled shoulders an aw-shucks shrug. His eyes were green as jade. "Mighty big city you got here, darlin'," he said, a drawl slipping into his voice.

"Oh—Ohio," the clerk repeated, like it was the most beautiful word she'd ever heard. She looked like she was unbuttoning his shirt with her eyes as she handed me the room key.

Very unprofessional, if you ask me.

But then again, how professional was it to check into a hotel with one of *Metropolitan*'s freelance writers—who, by the way, had obviously never even *been* to Ohio?

If he had, he'd have known they don't talk like cowboys there.

Michael Bishop lived on the Lower East Side of Manhattan; I lived on the Upper West Side. We'd known each other since our first years in the magazine business. Today we'd met for lunch, to go over a story he was writing for *Metropolitan*. The café, an elegant little French place with fantastic *jambon beurre* sandwiches, was close to my office.

It was also close to the Four Seasons.

We'd laughed, we'd had a glass of rosé—and now, suddenly, we were here.

*Am I really about to do this?*

"If you want tickets to a Broadway show or reservations at Rao's, the concierge can assist you," the clerk offered. By now she'd taken off Michael's shirt and was licking his chest.

"Actually," I said, "we have other plans." I grabbed Michael's hand and pulled him into the elevator before I lost my nerve.

We stood in front of our reflections in the gold-mirrored doors. "Really?" I said to mirror-Michael, who was as gorgeous as the real Michael but yellower. *"Ohio?"*

He laughed. "I know, Jane—you're a former fact-checker, so the truth is very important to you," he said. "I, however, am a writer, and I take occasional *liberties* with it." He stepped closer to me, and then he slipped an arm around my waist. "Nice dress, by the way," he said.

"Do you also take occasional liberties with your editors?" I asked, trying to be playful.

He shook his head. "Never," he said.

I believed him—but it didn't matter either way. This had been *my* idea.

It wasn't about loneliness, or even simple lust (though that obviously played a part). I just wanted to know if I could do something like this without feeling weird or cheap.

I still wasn't sure.

The hotel room was a gleaming, cream-colored box of understated luxury. A bottle of Chardonnay waited in a silver wine bucket, and there were gourmet chocolates arranged on the pillows. Through the giant windows, Manhattan glittered, a spectacle of steel and glass.

I stood in the center of the beautiful room, holding my purse against my body like a kind of shield. I was charged and excited and—all of a sudden—a little bit scared.

This was new territory for me. If I didn't turn tail and run right now, I was about to do something I'd barely even had the guts to imagine.

Michael, his green eyes both gentle and hungry, took the purse from my hands and placed it on a chair. Straightening up again, he brushed my hair away from my neck, and then he kissed me, gently, right above my collarbone. A shiver ran down my spine.

"Is this okay?" he asked softly.

I remembered the way he'd kissed my fingers at the café. I remembered how I'd said to him, *Let's get out of here.*

I wanted this.

"Yes," I breathed. "It's more than okay."

His lips moved up my neck, his tongue touching my skin ever so lightly. He traced a finger along my jawline and then slowly drew it down again, stopping at the low neckline of the Dress.

I waited, trembling, for him to slip his hand inside the silk.

But he didn't. He paused, barely breathing. And then he reached around my back and found the slender zipper between my shoulder blades. He gave it a sharp tug, and the black silk slid down my body in a whisper. I stood there—exposed, breathless, thrilled—and then Michael crushed his lips to mine.

We kissed deeply. Hungrily. I ran my palms up his strong arms, his broad shoulders. He reached under me and lifted me up, and I wrapped my legs around his waist. He tasted like wine.

I whispered my command: *"Take me to bed."* Then I added, "Please."

"So polite," he murmured into my hair. "Anything you say, Jane."

He carried me to the giant bed and laid me down on it. His fingers found my nipples through the lace of my bra, and then my bra, too, seemed to slip off my body, and his mouth was where his fingers had been.

I gasped.

*Yes, oh yes. I'm really doing this.*

His tongue teased me, pulled at me. His hands seemed to be everywhere at once. "Should I—" he began.

I said, "Don't talk, just do." I did not add *Please* this time.

I wriggled out of my panties as he undressed, and then he was naked before me, golden in the noon light, looking like some kind of Greek demigod descended from Mount Olympus.

I stretched up my arms and Michael fell into them. He kissed me again as I arched to meet him. When he thrust himself inside me, I cried out, rocking against his hips, kissing his shoulder, his neck, his chin. I pulled him into me with all my strength as the heat inside me rose in waves. When I cried out in release, my nails dug into Michael's shoulders. A moment later he cried out too, and then he collapsed on top of me, panting.

I couldn't believe it. I'd really done it.

Spent, we both slept for a little while. When I awoke, Michael was standing at the end of the bed, his shirt half buttoned, his golden chest still visible. A smile broke over his gorgeous face.

"Jane Avery, that was an incredible lunch," Michael Bishop said. "Could I interest you in dinner?"

I smiled back at him from the tangle of ivory sheets. As perfect as he was, as *this* had been, today was a one-time deal. I wasn't ready to get involved again. "Actually," I said, "thank you, but I have other plans."

He looked surprised. A guy like Michael wasn't used to being turned down. "Okay," he said after a moment. "I get it."

I doubted that he did.

*It's not you,* I thought, *it's me.*

After he kissed me good-bye—sweetly, longingly—I turned on the water in the deep porcelain tub. I'd paid seven hundred dollars for this room and I might as well enjoy it a little longer.

I sank into the bath, luxuriant with lavender-scented bubbles. It was crazy, what I'd done. But I'd loved it.

And I didn't feel cheap. *Au contraire:* I felt *rich.*

**I SWIPED A FREE** Perrier from the office fridge—one of the perks of working at *Metropolitan*—and hurried to my desk, only to find Brianne, my best friend and the magazine's ad sales director, draped dramatically across its cluttered surface.

"You took the looooongest lunch," she said accusingly. "We were supposed to get cappuccinos at Ground Central."

"I'm sorry," I said distractedly. I could see the message light on my phone blinking. "My meeting…um, my meeting didn't exactly go as planned. I'm going to have to work late tonight."

"Oh, *merde*." She gave a long, theatrical sigh. *"Pas encore."*

I couldn't help smiling. Brianne was one-quarter French; the rest of her was full-blown New Jersey. On a good day, she was funny and loud, as effervescent as a glass of Champagne; on a bad day she was like Napoleon with lipstick and PMS.

"Can we do it tomorrow?" I asked.

Bri still looked sulky. "You realize, don't you, that you stay late because you're avoiding your complete lack of a social life?"

"I stay because I care about my job." I tugged discreetly at my bra. Somehow I'd managed to put it on wrong.

"So do I," Bri said, "but you don't see me here at nine p.m. on a Friday."

"You're in a different department," I said, unwilling to admit that she had a point.

She took one of my blue editing pencils and twisted her pretty auburn hair around it, making an artfully messy bun. "I was going to set you up on a date tonight, you know."

"We've gone over this, Bri," I said firmly. "I'm not interested."

Bri lifted herself from my desk and stood before me with her hands on her hips. Five inches shorter than me, she had to crane her neck up. "I know how much you love your Netflix-and-Oreo nights, honey. But it's time you got back into the game."

I *did* love those nights, even though I'd be the first to admit that too many of them in a row got depressing. "I'm not ready to date, Bri. I like the sidelines."

Bri held up a manicured finger. "First of all, you've been divorced for almost a year and a half."

"Thanks for keeping track," I said.

Bri held up another finger. "Second of all, this guy's practically perfect."

"Then you date him," I suggested. "You're single now too. Aren't you? Or did you fall in love again last night?"

Bri giggled. She gave her heart away like it was candy on

Halloween. "There's the *cutest* guy in my spinning class," she admitted. She drifted off into a dreamy reverie for a moment. Then she shook her head and snapped back to attention. "Hey. You're changing the subject. We're talking about you and your nonexistent sex life."

A blush flared hot on my cheeks.

Bri immediately widened her eyes at me. Her mouth fell open, and then she nearly shouted, "Oh my God. You got laid last night!"

I looked wildly around. "Shhh!" I hissed. My boss's assistant was five feet away at the Xerox machine. She didn't seem to have heard Bri's accusation, though. Turning back to my friend, I made an effort to keep a straight face. To look serious and professional. "I did *not* get laid last night," I said.

*I got laid an hour ago.*

Bri's merry brown eyes grew narrow. "The more I look at you, the more I think there's something different about you today," she said.

I shrugged. "Well, I'm wearing a new dress." I gave a little twirl. "Isn't it fantastic?"

Bri's skeptical expression softened—but barely. "If you weren't the most honest person I've ever met, I'd swear you were lying to me, Jane Avery."

I smiled. "I'd never lie to you, hon," I said.

*But I might stretch the truth.*

"Are you sure you won't go out tonight?" she wheedled. "I want you to find a good man."

I sucked in my breath. My mood suddenly shifted. "I thought I had," I said.

Bri looked at me sympathetically. "I'm sorry you married a bastard, Janie. He fooled us all," she said. "But one error shouldn't ban you from the playing field."

I rubbed the spot where the big diamond ring used to be. James had loved me, he really had—but he'd also loved his ex-girlfriend. And her sister.

"Enough with the sports metaphors, Bri," I pleaded.

Bri mimed a baseball swing. "You gotta step up to the plate," she said, smirking, just to annoy me.

"And *you've* gotta get back to your own desk," I said, laughing. "I have work to do."

Bri walked reluctantly to the door and then turned back around. "Don't you want to know who your date was going to be?"

"Not really." I picked up my phone and pressed the messages button.

"Michael Bishop," she said as she walked away. "He is soooo handsome."

The receiver fell to my desk with a clunk.

*Step up to the plate, Bri?* I thought. *I did—and Michael Bishop was my home run.*

**WALKING INTO AL'S DINER** at 90th and Columbus after work that evening, I inhaled the familiar smell of grease and burned coffee—and underneath that, the subtle whiff of good olive oil, salty feta, and ripe heirloom tomatoes. My mouth watered as I slid into my familiar booth. Al's Diner looked like just another greasy spoon, but I knew its secret: *kolokitho keftedes* and *dolmades*—aka zucchini fritters and stuffed grape leaves—so delicious you'd swear you were on Santorini.

Al Dimitriou spotted me and lumbered out of the kitchen, wiping his hands on his stained apron. "Janie, *koreetsi mou,*" he said. *My girl.* "It's late! Either you already ate and you're here for baklava…or you worked too long and you're starving."

"Door number two," I said, smiling at him.

Al shook his head at me. "You work too hard, Jane-*itsa,*" he said. He turned and hollered, "Veta, Janie's here!"

"I know, I know!" Veta, Al's wife, came hurrying over with a basket of pita and a bowl of baba ghanoush. It took all my self-control to say *hello* and *thank you* before I started shoveling it into my mouth. Veta patted my head and gave me a quick maternal once-over. "You look very pretty tonight, Janie," she said. "Although the table manners…" She nudged me affectionately.

"Sorry," I mumbled. "Famished."

Al looked at me more carefully. "You got a date after this?"

*Why does everyone in New York City care about my dating life?*

"No such plans," I said, my mouth still full of warm pita and smoky eggplant.

Veta, who was as quick and petite as Al was big and slow, swatted him on his giant shoulder. "Just because she looks extra beautiful tonight doesn't mean she's going to see a man," she scolded. "Don't be so old-fashioned."

Al shrugged good-naturedly. "I was just making conversation."

"Just sticking your nose in a lady's business," Veta countered. She turned to me. "Don't mind the big lug," she said.

"I don't mind him," I said. "I love him."

At that, Al got slightly red and excused himself, saying something about needing to check on some fava beans.

Veta sat down across from me. She grinned. "So—do you?"

"Do I what?" I asked. I was having a hard time concentrating on anything other than the rich, delicious *meze*. I found an olive and popped it into my mouth.

"Have a date, you goose."

"No, Veta!" I exclaimed. "Why on earth—"

She ducked her head in embarrassment. "Sorry, sorry," she said. "I guess I was hoping."

"You don't need to hope for me," I said. "I'm happy."

And I was *very* happy right now. My God, the baba ghanoush…

Veta gazed thoughtfully out the window, where a flock of pigeons feasted on a discarded loaf of Wonder Bread. Then she turned back to me and said, "So, my happy Janie, do you want the lamb or the octopus?"

I laughed at her matter-of-factness. "Chef's choice," I said.

She patted my hand. "We'll take good care of you," she said.

"You always do," I said, because it was true.

It might have looked like I was sitting alone in a diner on a Friday night, but as far as I was concerned, I was having dinner with friends.

**BY THE TIME I** said good-bye to Al and Veta, night had fallen. Metal grates covered the doors of the Laundromat, the shoe boutique, and the store that specialized in four-hundred-dollar throw pillows. But cars and cabs still swept by on Columbus Avenue. Couples on dates strolled along, the women tottering in high, uncomfortable heels.

One of the benefits of being 5'8": you can just say no to stilettos.

As I stood on the corner, waiting to cross, I could see the light in my third-floor kitchen, burning small and yellow and alone.

*Netflix and Oreos, here I come,* I thought.

Just then, the wind caught the skirt of the Dress. The black silk seemed to swirl away from me, like there was a different direction it wanted to go in.

And why *should* I go home? I didn't have a dog or cat—I didn't even have a fish. The most I'd had was a cactus. (By the way, don't believe the hype about cacti: you *can* kill them, and it's not even hard.)

A little way down the block, the Teddy's Piano Bar sign blinked invitingly. The tiny watering hole had been there since the 1920s, when it was a speakeasy full of smoke and music, fueled by bathtub gin.

I'd never gone inside. But tonight, I walked straight toward it.

The walls were covered in abstract murals painted by some famous, long-dead artist. At the piano, a silver-haired man with a truly enormous nose played Gershwin. Couples chatted at small, cozy tables, and candlelight flickered on the murals, turning them into swirls of color and line.

I ordered a French 75 and sank into a banquette.

*"Summertime, and the livin' is easy,"* sang a black-haired beauty who'd joined the old man on the bench.

I smiled; I'd always loved that song. But I couldn't carry a tune in a Kate Spade handbag, so I hummed along quietly.

At the table next to me, a man sat alone with an unopened book and a glass of amber liquid. He'd taken off his tie and tucked it into the breast pocket of his gray linen suit. His fingers tapped along to the music.

I noted the lack of a wedding ring.

He had a good profile—deep-set eyes and a strong chin. I watched him out of the corner of my eye.

*Should I?* I thought. *I definitely shouldn't.*

But then I changed my mind.

I waited until the song had ended, and then I slid from the

banquette into the chair next to him. "Is this seat taken?" I asked.

The man looked up, startled. His dark eyebrows lifted. He smiled at me—a slow, almost shy smile. "I guess it is now," he said.

"I'm Jane," I said. "Hi."

"Hello, Jane, I'm Aiden," he said. He nodded toward my glass. "I'd buy you a drink, but you seem to have one already."

I clinked my cocktail to his and took a sip of the bubbly liquid. "You can buy the next round."

He laughed. "What if I bore you before that?"

I gave him my best mock-frown. "Don't tell me you have self-esteem problems, Aiden," I said. "You don't look the type."

He shrugged. "Let's just say I wasn't expecting a beautiful woman to sit down at my table tonight," he said.

*Please, I'm not beautiful*—that's what I almost said. But then I glanced down at my perfect, elegant Dress and felt a surge of confidence. What if, in calling me beautiful, Aiden was actually *right*? I smiled, sipped delicately at my drink, and made a new rule for myself: *If life hands you a compliment, take it.*

"This is a nice place," I said, looking around the dim, inviting room. "Do you come here often?" Then I felt like kicking myself for delivering such a cliché of a line.

Aiden swirled his whiskey and the ice clicked in the glass. "You could call me a regular, I guess. The guy at the piano is my uncle."

I looked at the homely silver-haired player again. "Hard to see the family resemblance," I said skeptically.

Aiden said, "Really? I think we look exactly alike."

"Aha! You *do* have a self-esteem problem," I said.

He grinned. "You have an understanding-sarcasm problem," he countered.

I laughed. I felt slightly tipsy, but it wasn't from the drink—I'd barely touched it. It was from being out on a Friday night and flirting with a handsome stranger.

I'd already done *one* thing I never thought I'd do today. Why stop there?

"So what do you do, Jane?" Aiden asked.

I shook my head. "Let's not talk about work."

Aiden looked disappointed. "You mean I don't get the chance to tell you about my fascinating work in maritime law?"

I leaned closer. "Do you prosecute pirates—with peg legs and hooks for hands?"

"If only," he said ruefully.

"Then I'm not interested." I sat back and crossed my arms. "You'll have to come up with a better topic for discussion."

Aiden laughed. "And now the beautiful woman makes conversational demands," he said.

I giggled. But I didn't let myself apologize.

And so this handsome stranger told me the story of his former cycling career, including the time he crashed on the Giro d'Italia, Italy's version of the Tour de France, and finished the day's race with a face dripping blood.

I liked the way he moved closer to me to tell it, the way he kept his voice low so he wouldn't disrupt his uncle's playing.

The song was "Memory," from *Cats,* and half the bar was mouthing the words.

I was allergic to cats. And *Cats*.

But I liked the feeling of Aiden's breath near my ear.

"—and then the race was momentarily stopped by cows in the road!" he was saying. "And the guy next to me is yelling *'Porca vacca!'* Which means 'pig cow,' literally, but also means 'damn it'—"

His face shone with the memory. He looked so happy and alive that before I knew what I was doing, I'd put my hand on top of his.

He stopped talking immediately. His eyes met mine, dark and questioning.

The room at the Four Seasons was mine until tomorrow at 11 a.m.

I knew that Aiden would go wherever I asked him to. Do whatever I wanted him to do.

He'd tell me cycling stories all night. Or serenade me while his uncle played John Lennon's "Imagine." Or he'd slip the Dress from my shoulders and make love to me until I was cross-eyed.

Wait a second: was I absolutely *insane?*

"Jane," he said, his voice suddenly husky.

I gazed into his dark eyes. My heart was thumping wildly.

I made a decision.

I said softly, "It's been so nice to meet you. But I have to go."

And then I picked up my handbag and dashed out of the bar. As I ran down the street, the strains of "The Music of the Night" faded behind me until I could hear nothing but the wind.

# JAMES PATTERSON

# BOOK**SHOTS**

## OUT THIS MONTH

### THE TRIAL: A WOMEN'S MURDER CLUB THRILLER

An accused killer will do anything to disrupt his own trial, including a courtroom shocker that Lindsay Boxer will never see coming.

### AIRPORT: CODE RED

A major terrorist cell sets a devastating plan in motion. Their target? One of the world's busiest airports.

### LITTLE BLACK DRESS

Can a little black dress change everything? What begins as one woman's fantasy is about to go too far.

### LEARNING TO RIDE

City girl Madeline Harper never wanted to love a cowboy. But rodeo king Tanner Callen might change her mind ... and win her heart.

# JAMES PATTERSON
# BOOKSHOTS
## COMING SOON

## CHASE: A MICHAEL BENNETT THRILLER

A man falls to his death in an apparent accident. But why does he have the fingerprints of another man who is already dead? Detective Michael Bennett is on the case.

## LET'S PLAY MAKE-BELIEVE

Christy and Marty just met, and it's love at first sight. Or is it? One of them is playing a dangerous game – and only one will survive.

## DEAD HEAT

Detective Carvalho is investigating the disappearance of an Australian athlete on the day of the opening ceremony of the 2016 Olympic Games. The case is about to take a deadly turn…

## THE McCULLAGH INN IN MAINE

Chelsea O'Kane escapes to Maine to build a new life – until she runs into Jeremy Holland, an old flame…

# ALSO BY JAMES PATTERSON

### ALEX CROSS NOVELS

Along Came a Spider
Kiss the Girls
Jack and Jill
Cat and Mouse
Pop Goes the Weasel
Roses are Red
Violets are Blue
Four Blind Mice
The Big Bad Wolf
London Bridges
Mary, Mary
Cross
Double Cross
Cross Country
Alex Cross's Trial (*with Richard DiLallo*)
I, Alex Cross
Cross Fire
Kill Alex Cross
Merry Christmas, Alex Cross
Alex Cross, Run
Cross My Heart
Hope to Die
Cross Justice

### THE WOMEN'S MURDER CLUB SERIES

1st to Die
2nd Chance (*with Andrew Gross*)
3rd Degree (*with Andrew Gross*)
4th of July (*with Maxine Paetro*)

The 5th Horseman (*with Maxine Paetro*)
The 6th Target (*with Maxine Paetro*)
7th Heaven (*with Maxine Paetro*)
8th Confession (*with Maxine Paetro*)
9th Judgement (*with Maxine Paetro*)
10th Anniversary (*with Maxine Paetro*)
11th Hour (*with Maxine Paetro*)
12th of Never (*with Maxine Paetro*)
Unlucky 13 (*with Maxine Paetro*)
14th Deadly Sin (*with Maxine Paetro*)
15th Affair (*with Maxine Paetro*)

### DETECTIVE MICHAEL BENNETT SERIES

Step on a Crack (*with Michael Ledwidge*)
Run for Your Life (*with Michael Ledwidge*)
Worst Case (*with Michael Ledwidge*)
Tick Tock (*with Michael Ledwidge*)
I, Michael Bennett (*with Michael Ledwidge*)
Gone (*with Michael Ledwidge*)
Burn (*with Michael Ledwidge*)
Alert (*with Michael Ledwidge*)

### PRIVATE NOVELS

Private (*with Maxine Paetro*)
Private London (*with Mark Pearson*)
Private Games (*with Mark Sullivan*)
Private: No. 1 Suspect (*with Maxine Paetro*)

Private Berlin (*with Mark Sullivan*)

Private Down Under (*with Michael White*)

Private L.A. (*with Mark Sullivan*)

Private India (*with Ashwin Sanghi*)

Private Vegas (*with Maxine Paetro*)

Private Sydney (*with Kathryn Fox*)

Private Paris (*with Mark Sullivan*)

The Games (*with Mark Sullivan*)

### NYPD RED SERIES

NYPD Red (*with Marshall Karp*)

NYPD Red 2 (*with Marshall Karp*)

NYPD Red 3 (*with Marshall Karp*)

NYPD Red 4 (*with Marshall Karp*)

### STAND-ALONE THRILLERS

Sail (*with Howard Roughan*)

Swimsuit (*with Maxine Paetro*)

Don't Blink (*with Howard Roughan*)

Postcard Killers (*with Liza Marklund*)

Toys (*with Neil McMahon*)

Now You See Her (*with Michael Ledwidge*)

Kill Me If You Can (*with Marshall Karp*)

Guilty Wives (*with David Ellis*)

Zoo (*with Michael Ledwidge*)

Second Honeymoon (*with Howard Roughan*)

Mistress (*with David Ellis*)

Invisible (*with David Ellis*)

The Thomas Berryman Number

Truth or Die (*with Howard Roughan*)

Murder House (*with David Ellis*)

### NON-FICTION

Torn Apart (*with Hal and Cory Friedman*)

The Murder of King Tut (*with Martin Dugard*)

### ROMANCE

Sundays at Tiffany's (*with Gabrielle Charbonnet*)

The Christmas Wedding (*with Richard DiLallo*)

First Love (*with Emily Raymond*)

### OTHER TITLES

Miracle at Augusta (*with Peter de Jonge*)

### BOOKSHOTS

Black & Blue (*with Candice Fox*)

Break Point (*with Lee Stone*)

Cross Kill

Private Royals (*with Rees Jones*)

The Hostage (*with Robert Gold*)

Zoo 2 (*with Max DiLallo*)

Heist (*with Rees Jones*)

Hunted (*with Andrew Holmes*)